A TON OF TROUBLE

Also by Lynne Murray

At Large
Large Target
Larger Than Death

A TON OF TROUBLE

A JOSEPHINE FULLER MYSTERY

Lynne Murray

St. Martin's Minotaur ≈ New York

ISBN 0-312-30077-8

First Edition: July 2002

10 9 8 7 6 5 4 3 2 1

This book is dedicated to
all those people whose beauty is writ large
and their admirers of whatever size.
May you flower in abundance,
unmoved by the efforts of the small-minded
to contain, constrain, or belittle.

Acknowledgments

Maurice Newburn generously volunteered to run the sort of adult establishment described as Newburn's Blue Movies. The real M. C. Newburn Books in Albany, California, is home to Tricky—the CEO, Cat Everybody Obeys. The real Newburn's carries books for all ages and welcomes adults and minors alike. No dogs, though—Tricky is very strict on that point.

Ann Dugger's suggestion in regard to wine barrel contents was extremely helpful, and Josephine's initial reaction is a direct quote from Ann.

Thanks to Sarah Kennedy of the Video Production Team at Good Vibrations in San Francisco, www.goodvibes.com, for ideas about what adult videos are and what they could be.

I very much appreciate the help of Yohannon of www.rotunda.com in offering personal and philosophical observations on adult films, including previously unknown piña colada lore.

I greatly appreciate Jerry Gardner's describing his experiences as a still photographer on an adult film set.

Particular thanks to Jonathon Eros for checking the Sonoma County locations, vegetation, and travel routes.

Thanks to Christopher Rankin and Simon Berry for providing some of the more brilliant fragments of observation and opinion in this mosaic.

I want to express my personal gratitude to some people who made a material difference in my survival during the time of writing this book—Jacqueline Stone, David Wigginton, Cheri Jamison, Adam Goldberg, Jaqueline Girdner, and Gregory Booi—thank you.

T he letter from Wolf Lambert looked like the answer to a maiden's prayer, if the maiden happened to be sexually frustrated and trying hard to be a good sport in a situation where she felt like the spare tire on a tricycle. Okay, I admit there was a glimmer of Hollywood glamour around the guy. Wolf had directed some spectacularly successful horror films, and he was charismatic, even now—after he had retired to devote himself to his passions of making wine and adult films about large women. At well over two hundred pounds, I qualify as a large woman, and Wolf had not been shy about expressing his admiration, which I found flattering but amusing rather than arousing. I had last seen him cavorting in a hot tub with his assistant, Thelma, who qualified as a supersized woman. I had not been tempted to accept their invitation to join the two of them in hot water, but I couldn't help having a certain sneaking admiration for their uninhibited ways.

Written on the rich cream-colored stationery of Wolf's Lambert's Lair Winery, topped by the drawing of his wine labels—a purple-ink sketch of a lamb and wolf curled up cozily—the note itself was penned in blue ink with calligraphic script. The contents took a sharp left turn from the presentation:

Dear former friend, business associate, ex-wife, or lover,

I am writing to make amends. Sobriety is a very new state for me and I want to do this 12-step thing correctly. Some of the details of how badly I treated you are lost from my memory, but I am sure you recall them. You may not be able to find it in your heart to forgive me, but I do apologize.

Sincerely,
Wolf Lambert

P.S. The winery will be open for tastings from 10:00 to 4:00 every day during October. Please do come visit us.

The postscript appeared to demonstrate that the man who had become famous making horror films was a little unclear on the whole sobriety part of the recovery program. I had met him on two occasions now, and he hadn't been remotely sober either time. Still, it was an invitation to the wine country, and the least I could do was assure Wolf that as far as I was concerned there was no hurt to mend.

The October weather was sunny, Indian summer in San Francisco, but I had brought my own fog of yearning. I started a new assignment in that city on Monday, but I arrived two days early because of a man named Mulligan, who happened to be attending a security convention at the Moscone Center over the weekend.

He lived in the apartment below me back in Seattle, but somehow it was very hard to negotiate that stairway.

This weekend, he had told me he would be staying at a

hotel near the convention center, south of Market Street. I had called him to see if he had time for lunch, since we were in the same town. He said he would meet me in front of the Moscone Center at 1:00 P.M. Was I making a fool of myself over a man? Probably. Hey, everyone needs a hobby.

I went straight from the airport to my employer's Jackson Heights mansion overlooking San Francisco Bay. Mrs. Madrone's personal assistant, Ambrose Terrell, answered the door. Tall enough to look down his nose at most of the world, lean and red haired.

"I don't think I've ever seen you so informally dressed." I tilted my head up to make eye contact. His shirt front was immaculate, pale blue with stripes darker blue than his eyes. His trousers were tailored but khaki.

"I'll be off duty for the weekend as soon as Mrs. Madrone goes out."

"You know if I ever saw you in blue jeans I think I'd faint," I said as he ushered me up the impressive staircase.

He nodded serenely. "That's been known to happen in certain neighborhoods of this very city."

"I didn't mean it that way. Although I'm sure you get wolf whistles."

"That, too."

He opened the door and waited while Mrs. Madrone turned her wheelchair away from watching the morning sunlight and sailboats on the bright blue waters sliding under the

Golden Gate Bridge. For once Ambrose seemed uncertain whether she wanted him to go or stay.

"You're two days early Jo, and I haven't much time this morning. Ambrose, make arrangements for the car, I'm going to that luncheon, after all."

When Ambrose had departed, Mrs. Madrone gestured me in. Prince, her lilac point Siamese, blinked at me from his cozy perch in a spot of sunlight on Mrs. Madrone's huge Mission-style desk—no doubt procured with a special dispensation from an actual Mission.

"Ambrose has a list of places I'd like you to look in on here in the Bay Area."

"Yes, ma'am."

"Don't let them know we're even considering giving them a grant. But tell me what you can find out about them and if you think they're doing something worth supporting. I'll be in Paris next week, but Ambrose will be here. And do try not to get into trouble this time, Josephine. I have a lot of friends in this town and I'd hate to have them amused by gossip at my expense."

I looked for a smile on her narrow pale face and failed to find one. "I haven't been arrested so far, Mrs. Madrone."

She unbent enough to smile. "Well, thank heaven for small favors." She wheeled her chair around and headed for a door into an adjoining room. The interview was over.

On my way out I nearly ran into Ambrose, who had a smile on his face. "Are you off now?" I asked.

"Just about to go, but here's the folder for the group Mrs. Madrone wants you to look into, and a letter that just came in for you." He handed me the folder and a letter with the Lambert's Lair return address. But before I could turn to go, he said. "Wait." He waved an additional envelope under my nose. "I wanted a word with you. I have you booked into the Pine Street corporate condo, or should I try to reach you with Mulligan at his hotel this weekend?"

"You know everything."

"Not quite, or I wouldn't be asking."

"The short answer is, I don't know."

"Well, then here are the keys to the Pine Street place. But I have something else that might interest you."

"Does this explain the cat-licking-its-whiskers expression on your face?"

"Be quiet, Jo, I'm about to do something nice for you, so don't screw it up." He handed me a key and a brochure. "This is a reservation for tonight and tomorrow night at Valley of the Moon Cottage. Their advance reservation rate is twice a regular hotel's rate, but even getting the reservation is impossible this time of year."

"What is the Valley of the Moon Cottage?"

"It's a guest house not far from the old Jack London estate. It's just one cottage on a couple acres of land. There's a creek, a few hiking trails, and a hot tub with a view of a little private garden. It feels more isolated than it actually is. They stock breakfast food and you can drive to Glen Ellen if you feel like fine dining."

I just stared at him.

"It's not a gift because you'd have to pay the room rate, but if you want a romantic getaway, it's ideal. It's more reasonable because we made the reservations so far in advance. There's a waiting list."

"You can't use it?"

"I had to make the reservation early, but a certain gentleman was urgently called out of town on business. If you don't

6

want it, there are several other people I could give it to."

"No, thanks, I'll take it. How much is it?"

He told me and I nodded. It wasn't bad considering the location and the hot tub. "That's so kind of you, Ambrose. I'm sorry your own plans didn't work out."

"Don't worry, I've got several old acquaintances to catch up with here in the City." He patted me on the shoulder, "At least it won't go to waste—call them if you have to check in late."

"Okay." Sharing a romantic cottage with Mulligan would be nice, but even if I ended up alone there—the hot tub appealed to me.

I met Mulligan outside the massive Moscone Center. He was easy to spot—standing still, taller than most of the throngs of badge-wearing convention-goers, he had longish blond hair and the face of a discontented bulldog. I had seen him just two days earlier when we were both arranging with the building manager, Maxine, to feed our respective cats. Somehow the brisk sunshine of an October day in San Francisco inspired us to hug hello. I restrained my impulse to unpin my hair and take off my business-like blazer.

We walked over to the Cadillac Bar and Grill, a cavernous Mexican restaurant on an alley off Fourth Street. It had tile-topped tables and a couple of television sets over the bar. Even with the convention in town, we found a table. The food was good and a couple of Dos Equis lowered the tension level.

"Do you think the cats will be okay together in Nina's, I mean, my place." I was still coming to terms with my late friend's apartment being mine. Along with the cat and the apartment building, Thor Mulligan had been Nina's, too, and she had been gone five months now.

"When I last saw them, they were cuddled up together on the sofa." Mulligan smiled.

The eye contact lasted long enough to make me feel shy all at once. "They've been doing that." We both finished our beers and ordered seconds. I took off the blazer.

Raoul, the cat who could say his own name, was a huge gray Persian I had inherited from Nina. Then a few months ago, Mulligan had brought home a little black bundle of fur and curiosity he named La Niña. Dismayed by the tiny kitten, Raoul had hissed and retreated throughout the first day every time she bounced up to say hello. It had taken two days before he consented to stretch out his head, and touch noses with her.

Then he had licked the top of her head, around her ears, and finally all over. By the end of the day they wound up curled around each other like a yin-yang symbol.

Mulligan and I had come close to that degree of intimacy for one passionate encounter a few months earlier. But after that he had backed away. Over the next few months we had been getting to know each other tentatively. We lingered over another beer. Being together in a strange city seemed to bring us closer.

We walked back to his hotel with crowds of lunching office workers shouldering past us. "Want to come up for a moment?" He took my hand.

"Okay." I hadn't got round to telling him about the reservation in Sonoma.

Mulligan's room seemed nice. I had a vague impression of dusty rose and maroon walls, curtains, and bedspread before he closed the door by pressing me up against it in an urgent kiss that I returned with interest and a sigh of relief as the last few months of cautious distance seemed to dissolve. I did unpin my hair. We wound up in very short order sprawled on the hotel bed and seriously approaching the yin-yang stage when a hammering at the door was followed by a man's voice yelling. "Open up, it's the police."

O h, come on!" was my reaction.

But Mulligan got up and we both adjusted our clothing, and I pulled the rumpled covers back over the bed while
he went to look out the peephole and open the door. Two men
burst into the room. For some reason I thought of Yogi Bear
and his smaller buddy, Boo Boo. It must have been the pork-
pie hat and short tie on the larger one and the smaller one's
air of looking around the room as if jelly donuts were stashed
somewhere.

The larger man was about six feet tall and Mulligan's age,
maybe a little older, with gray stubble on his cheeks, receding
salt-and-pepper hair, and a strong odor of stale coffee, as if
he had spritzed some on as an aftershave. He wore a shirt and
tie and a baggy sport coat with a tweed pattern that alternated
between pavement gray and pond scum green. His companion,
a head shorter, light-skinned African American, with gray-
streaked hair cut very short, glanced around the hotel room
as if he were memorizing it. He wore a sport coat in a brown-
beige herringbone pattern over an open-necked polo shirt—
no hat. Both men had the air of just having been released
from a rehab facility and handed clothing from a charitable
thrift store bin on the way out.

Mulligan was ecstatic to see them. Sure enough, old army buddies. The one I thought of as Yogi was actually named Harvey, and Boo Boo was Wally. They had gone from the army into the security business. I stifled a sigh. Meeting these guys was the main purpose of the trip. Mulligan would be preoccupied.

I walked them back to the convention center. Harvey and Wally were both divorced. No big surprise there. They had not brought along any womenfolk for this weekend. They were scrupulously polite to me, although my guess was that they preferred the other type of woman—the warm, welcoming, flirtatious, and preferably not-too-bright type. With my size and Mulligan being both tall and broad, I halfway expected them to attempt some "mating season among the large mammals" joke. But they weren't about to do so in front of a lady. I was fervently hoping it would be unnecessary to prove myself anything other than a lady in their presence.

They were sure they could get me into the trade show on an extra badge, and I was tempted for a moment. Then they started describing some of the high-tech highlights they were anticipating. I took Mulligan aside and told him perhaps I'd better go check into the corporate condo. His eyes were half on his friends and he didn't say anything about offering me accommodation. He did give me his pager number and suggest that I join the three of them for dinner and drinks. Harvey and Wally were located in the Bay Area and they knew a great steak place.

As I said farewell for the moment, the taller one, Harvey, pulled out a tiny camera and enlisted me to take pictures of the three of them standing in front of the Moscone Center entrance, where their convention was listed on a marquee. I snapped a few pictures of them. Then Mulligan gave me such a passionate kiss good-bye that I stood a moment, stunned. The three men headed through the glass door, Mulligan sketching a wave with a smug expression on his face and the other two earnestly discussing some hypersensitive listening device.

It was several seconds after they passed from view before I realized that they had left the tiny camera with me. Oh, well, I could give it back over dinner. I dropped it in my purse and went to get my car.

I checked into the corporate condo on Pine, but I was restless. I walked down Pine into the Financial District to clear my head from the beer and the last lingering mists of lust. At last I found a café on Pine and Kearny and sat at a table by the window with a latte while I opened up the letter that Ambrose had handed me.

Wolf Lambert's apology and invitation made the decision for me. I had no idea what he was apologizing for. Perhaps he had confused me with someone else. The idea of a reformed Wolf Lambert intrigued me, even though the odds were a little long. But visiting Wolf gave me an excuse to drive up to Sonoma County instead of skulking around San Francisco feeling rejected.

I opened up a wine country map and discovered that the Lambert's Lair Winery was not far away from the Valley of the Moon Cottage, between one and two hours' drive north of San Francisco. I could drive up, look in on Wolf, and check into the cottage. Then maybe I would just page Mulligan from there and let him know where he could find me when he had finished his male bonding.

I left my bags at the corporate condo, grabbed a toothbrush, a change of clothes, and the Valley of the Moon reservation, then retrieved the rental car and headed north, across the Golden Gate Bridge. If I were overcome by a shameful, yet irresistible, urge to rush back to Mulligan's side, I could be there in a few hours for a steak dinner with him and the bad news bears, and an evening filled with enough chatter on the latest security devices to atone for my sins in this, and perhaps a few other, lifetimes.

It was even hotter in Sonoma County than it had been in
San Francisco. In Baronsville it was eighty-something, but
it lacked the fertile viney smell I had noticed in August just
before the harvest. The vineyards, stripped of their grapes,
seemed to shrink in on themselves, ready to slip into their
dormant phase as soon as the winter weather would let them.
I was able to find the winery easily enough. The gates with
their Lambert's Lair sign stood open—the lamb and wolf logo
re-created in wrought iron over the sign. Tour and tasting
schedules were posted. The place had been tidied up since
my last visit. The bird droppings and tree sap had been
washed off the intercom. The gravel in the road looked fresh
and the parking lot was raked as if in anticipation of visitors,
but only two cars were parked in front of the building. One
was a dust-covered Mercedes station wagon, the other an even
dustier blue Toyota Corolla.

   I went in the door, hoping to run into the bookkeeper,
Thelma, last seen cavorting with an impressive display of
supersized flesh, in a hot tub with Wolf Lambert. But a slender
young woman was sitting on a chair behind the counter watching a soap opera on a portable television set. She must have
been in her late teens and she had heavy-lidded brown eyes

and sensual full lips that gave her face a knowing air that contrasted with her uncertainty when she saw me come in.

She tapped a remote with elegantly manicured nails and reluctantly turned to face me. "Can I help you?"

I waved the letter, "I got this letter and I happened to be in town, so I thought I'd come by. The sign at the gate said there were tours at one-thirty and three-thirty."

She didn't seem curious about the letter. She sighed, "You aren't a *Restless Hearts* fan are you?"

"Is that a soap opera?"

"Yeah." Her eyes kept sliding back to the screen. "When no one came by one-twenty, I thought maybe I could watch it." There was a pleading tone to her voice. "It'll be over by two, would you mind waiting? I mean because it's not like there's a whole group."

"Not at all, I'll just poke around and look at the vines till you're done."

She hit the volume on the television remote and the organ music swelled, under the actors' emotion-charged voices. "Thanks." She turned back, instantly absorbed by the action on the screen.

I went back out, just as glad not to have her come along with me. I had liked Thelma, and Wolf had a certain drunken, horny charm. This girl no doubt sold wine by the crate to men wandering into the tasting room, but her disinterest in me was palpable, and I could tell already that I wasn't going to find her conversation riveting.

I had seen the deck at the back of the house on my previous visit, no sign of Wolf and Thelma back there today. The hot tub had some kind of plastic cover over it. Behind the house on a gently rising hill was a weathered barnlike structure, with a taller, square-built modern warehouse next to it.

Home to the actual wine-making machinery, no doubt.

I walked all the way around the house itself to a parking lot annex that wasn't visible from the front. Before I could complete the circuit to wind up in front of the tasting-room door again, I encountered an unfinished wood table that stood in front of a stack of empty wine barrels and half barrels balanced on their sides in an unstable-looking pyramid. A hand-lettered sign taped to a barrel identified them as "Wine Barrel Planters for Sale—$50." Half barrels went for twenty-five dollars.

A striped canvas awning provided shade over the table, but no one sat in the folding chair behind it. I envisioned the table stocked with bigger souvenirs on a day with more visitors, and a crowd spilling out of the tasting room would be milling around the grounds and buying. I poked around the stack of wine barrels, wondering if my friend Maxine, who had taken over Nina's backyard rose garden, would like a half-barrel planter. The whole barrels looked unwieldy.

I turned back toward the house. A brand new BMW pulled up and two couples got out. I followed them into the tasting room. The television noise was instantly cut off. I watched from the doorway as the young woman set up a selection of wines to be tasted. She smiled, and was wisely agreeing with everything the BMW driver said. She did have the instinct to let him show off his wine expertise. I couldn't find an opening to ask about Wolf or Thelma. As Mr. BMW began to expound on the hint of vanilla in the nose of the Chardonnay I went back out again.

The pre-harvest viney smell I remembered from my visit in August had surrendered to a smoky fall smell. Someone was burning leaves or wood not too far away. The road wound off around the hill and the main house disappeared from view.

At the top of a long rise, I could see a steeper hill with a lush, cultivated lawn on top. The golden beige of the surrounding hills testified that shade trees and green grass were foreign to this landscape. A lawn like that would have to be nurtured, watered, and tended. The road winding up to the hilltop started low enough that the rolling hills planted with grapevines disappeared from view behind eucalyptus, manzanita, scrub, and live oak. This part of the property was a dusty dirt track bounded by bushes and trees.

A low, growling motor could be heard around the next curve and a dark gray Jaguar came into view, driving cautiously on the deep ruts that were the road. Even the leaping cat chrome hood ornament was coated with the dust that rose around it in a cloud. The road was narrow enough that although I stood on the dirt furrow of a shoulder, pressed up against the border of bushes, the car moved past almost close enough to touch. I cursed softly, hoping that the bush I was standing in wasn't poison oak.

The driver was a gray-haired, olive-skinned man with a hawklike profile. He turned to look me up and down for a second, with the air of a man considering a particularly uninformative road sign. Then he returned his gaze to the road ahead, winding up to the main house.

The passenger, a much younger man, had the opposite coloration—arctic blue eyes and blond hair, cut short enough to stand up like a brush. He was burly enough that he seemed crammed into the luxurious sports car. His pale eyes fixed on the windshield. The man at the wheel said something and the blond passenger turned his eyes on me with a calculating stare. A trained attack dog looked at me like that once— estimating the distance from jaws to target, waiting for the word of command to leap at it.

A Ton of Trouble

This was an interior road on Wolf Lambert's winery property. Those guys didn't strike me as the lost tourist type. I wondered if they were somehow related to Wolf. Visitors? Houseguests? Business associates who had just come to make him an offer he couldn't refuse?

5

When I reached the top of the hill I could look down on all the vineyards and rolling hills of Wolf's property. The flattened lawn up here had been cultivated for public events. A rustic border of whitewashed rocks marched around edges of the manicured grass and concluded in front of a dirt turnaround that might have served as a small parking lot as well. A couple of incongruous blue plastic Port-a-Potties stood there, just where the rocks ended. The place was deserted. No cars in the lot and everything was orderly, as if recently tidied up, with the exception of an oddly out-of-place rock a little smaller than the whitewashed border rocks. I probably wouldn't have noticed it if it hadn't been right in front of the blue plastic stall, where anyone going in or out would trip over it. The Jaguar must have been up here. They might have gone up to use the Port-a-Pottie, but somehow those guys hadn't seemed to be shy types who go out of their way to avoid peeing on the odd roadside bush.

The lawn was shaded by eucalyptus and oak trees and had been cultivated as a small park with an elevated ornate white gazebo at one end. It was a pleasant spot. I walked over to the other side to see what the view was like from there. Rolling hills covered with rows of grapevines, climbing their chest-high trellises. The paths between the rows gave the hills a striped look.

A scrap of paper fluttered in a light breeze, caught against the edge of a white painted step up to the little round floor of the gazebo. I picked up the paper and glanced around. The grassy area was clear of anything else in the way of litter. No discarded cigarette butts, paper cups, or fast-food wrappers. I walked up the two steps to the gazebo and sat down on the white bench that ringed the edge of it.

I opened up the paper. It was a sheet of the same heavy cream-colored Lambert's Lair stationery as the letter from Wolf. But the handwriting was as different as could be from that elegant calligraphy. This was an untidy scrawl—after a few lines the scribbles resolved themselves into names.

> *Gloria, Anita, Teri, Jeff, Ivan, 1983–86 Cheryl and Maria???, Lillian, Mandy, Art, Sylvia, Angie— more?*

I shrugged and put the paper in my pocket. The portable latrines were the closest thing around to a trash basket, and I didn't feel like either walking over there to dispose of it or putting it back on the ground to litter the immaculate grass. I looked out over the peaceful rolling hills, and could see the back deck of the main house, the former barn behind it, and farther up the hill, the warehouse building. The back door of the house opened and I saw Thelma—Wolf's bookkeeper and hot tub partner—come out onto the deck. Even though her bright red hair was hidden under a broad-brimmed straw hat, her size made her easy to identify. She was one of the largest women I had ever seen. She moved slowly toward the redwood tub and settled down onto the stone bench beside it.

Had she been in the house all along? It was possible. She might be living there for all I knew. I hadn't seen her drive up. I turned back to scan the parking lot and saw a late-model sport-utility vehicle next to the BMW. This was one of those hulking black Darth Vader models. A man built along the same scale as the vehicle stood beside it, his arms crossed, staring at the gravel below his feet. Suddenly, as if he knew I was watching, he looked up. It must have been an illusion because it was unlikely that he would have seen me from that distance, but he seemed to meet my eyes and I almost wanted to hide for some odd reason. He leaned into the driver's-side window and said something to the driver, who was blocked from my vision.

Meanwhile, on the back deck I could see Thelma on the stone bench next to the tub, reaching round behind the shrouded hot tub. She had a tote bag over her arm and she began to transfer small objects one by one from behind the tub into the bag. It was too far away to identify what she was picking up.

I decided to see if I could catch up to her. I began to hurry down the dusty path. There was a finality about the way she was packing the canvas tote that gave me the feeling she was departing and I might not get to talk to her again. She was such a good-humored person that I had liked her in our first encounter. She also had a vulnerability about her that made me worry for her, without quite knowing why. Perhaps because of the extra ration of prejudice that she could hardly avoid. Coping at my size wasn't easy and at her size it was bound to be that much more difficult.

No sense denying that I was also a bit mystified by how such an intelligent woman could be so enthusiastically involved in making adult films. Wolf Lambert was charming, but the old lecher couldn't be paying her *that* much. By the time I reached the parking lot, she was being helped into the passenger side of the SUV by the square-built dark-haired man. The man behind the wheel—also dark haired—turned his head toward me. I could see he wore mirrored sunglasses. As I got closer, I was more impressed by the size of the man standing next to Thelma. This guy was not fat, but so muscular that he was almost in proportion with the supersized Thelma. He had slid the back door open and was climbing in.

"Thelma!" I called, breathless from half jogging down the hill.

She heard me and said something to the driver, who turned the engine off.

"Just a minute, Rod." Thelma said, "I remember her from before." She rolled down the window and the muscular man leaned against the door and looked at me carefully. "Don't worry, boys," Thelma said, "She's okay. She came to see Wolf a few months ago. I forget your name though." She held out a hand with long red nails.

"Josephine Fuller," I said, gasping. We shook hands and I stood by, catching my breath.

She gestured to the man leaning against the open back door, "This is Rod Manx—you may not be able to tell him from his brother Ringo. They're twins." She giggled irrepressibly. "Double the pleasure—well, you saw them in the films."

I let that go past, and shook hands with Rod Manx. Ringo, the driver, leaned across Thelma's lap, close enough that I could see my reflection in his sunglasses, and briefly touched my hand. I noticed that he wore a ring on every finger.

"Unusual names." I forced myself to look away from my reflection in Ringo's glasses.

Rod smiled, "Nom de porn. No one could ever pronounce

our real last name, anyway. You can guess why I picked Rod. Although there are a few other Rods in the porn business." Both Manx brothers and Thelma laughed.

I smiled good-naturedly, although it didn't quite merit a laugh in my book.

"Anyway," Rod said, smiling genially, "Ringo likes to wear jewelry, and he's got a different pair of shades for every outfit." Rod tilted his head toward the man in the driver's seat, but his eyes never left mine. "That's a way to tell us apart."

"That and the birthmark," Ringo said.

The three of them laughed again.

"Can't miss that birthmark, can you? Isn't that fun?" Thelma's bubbly enthusiasm was flowing now. "That name Manx gave me the idea for the video we're shooting tomorrow," she trilled. "It's Scottish—I've got kilts, bagpipes, it's wonderful."

"Uh, but Manx would be from the Isle of Man. That's not exactly Scottish is it?" I was confused.

"Oh, it's not about geography, honey," her voice slid down an octave and suddenly she was imitating Mae West.

The imitation was lost on Rod, who shrugged. Ringo, though he was facing forward and couldn't see his brother, shrugged the identical way and at the exact same moment.

I cleared my throat. "I was in town with my friend at a convention, but I got this strange letter from Wolf—"

Thelma nodded. "Say no more, dear. We all got them."

"Who is 'we'?"

"Most of the people in Wolf's address book. It's all Heather's fault."

"Let me guess, the girl who watches soap operas between wine-tasting guests."

"That's Heather. She's such an airhead. I don't see how

Wolf could imagine that she could do invitations without any supervision. She does have lovely handwriting, but she's not capable of writing and thinking at the same time. She got hold of the draft Wolf was making of some kind of amends letter for his twelve-step program and she sent it out to most of the people in his address book, along with the fall invitations to visit the tasting room." Thelma shook her head, while the Manx brothers smiled patiently.

"Is the winery getting a lot of calls?"

Thelma laughed, "Heather is answering the phones and taking most of the messages, so most of them get lost. Sometimes the winemaster's daughter, Sylvia, answers the phone. Last time I asked, she said there have been quite a few complaints. Of course, Heather didn't keep a list of who she sent them to, so Wolf won't know till all the protests roll in. Maybe then he can get an idea where she stopped. They took her stationery away and put her back selling wine."

"All this about recovery—has Wolf seriously quit drinking?"

Thelma sighed. "I've known him five years and every year about this time he quits. This time he is attending AA meetings in town. But you know, honey, the Overeaters Anonymous meetings are in the same building at the same time, and he might be cruising the local talent."

Ringo started to laugh, and Thelma turned and hit him lightly on the arm. "It's true!"

"We know that," Rod said. Ringo tilted his head at me from the driver's seat and both men favored me with the identical professionally charming smile. Except for the sunglasses it would have been synchronized seduction. Perhaps that was their Olympic event.

Thelma looked from Rod to Ringo and back to me, beaming with a benevolent air. I remembered her efforts to get me to strip down and jump into the hot tub.

Thelma laughed again. "Every year so far, Wolfie has always started up drinking again in time for the holidays, so we'll see. He might be more serious this time. He told me his doctor put him on that drug that keeps you from drinking, what's it called?"

"Antabuse?" I asked.

"I think that's it. Between you and me, Wolfie's drinking was starting to have an effect in the," she lowered her voice, "performance department, if you get my drift."

Rod, chuckled, and Ringo, from the driver's seat, turned back to grin at his brother.

"The guys are smiling because that's their area of expertise."

"I beg your pardon?"

"You don't recognize them with their clothes on do you?"

"What?"

"Oh, don't tell me you never got the catalog. I'm sure I sent you one. Well, maybe I slipped up. Things have been a little hectic here. Once I moved out—forget it. Anyway I'm getting the impression you haven't seen our films. Rod and Ringo have made over a hundred adult videos of all kinds. They've done a few dozen just for Wolf, and now I'm lucky to have them for the next two days to do my first video."

"Uh, Thelma, this is all new to me. I thought you worked for Wolf—you were his bookkeeper and did the um, films, as a sideline."

"Well, things have changed since last we met. Wolf and I are still dear friends, but I couldn't handle his, well, let's say his disorganization. The drinking was part of it, but it was worse than that. So I've moved on. I've put together my own company. We have backers and a script. We start filming this weekend on our first video. It's called *A Ton of Trouble*."

"You're in it?"

"Yes, writing it, directing it, starring in it. I do it all."

This last remark caused all three of them to laugh again.

"And I have five other large women in it, so it really does add up to about a ton."

"Uh-huh."

"Want to see the filming?"

Something possessed me to ask, "Uh, can I bring my boyfriend?" I started to blush.

"That is so cute. Of course you can. Isn't she sweet, Rod? And if you two are inspired, there's always room for more to join in."

Now I was really blushing, and regretted asking. But Thelma was unabashed. She handed me a purple card that read "Thelma T, Director/Producer/Star—Ton of Fun Productions," with a post office box and a telephone number. "Call the number tomorrow and I'll give you directions. I don't like to give out the address where we're shooting in advance for security reasons."

I looked up and noticed that Rod Manx was examining me from head to foot. I refused to let that intimidate me, but I did wonder if he had seen me up on the hilltop watching him.

"I can see you're taken with Rod. Wait till you see the two brothers in action."

"Uh, so is Wolf in some kind of rehab facility?" I asked, as Rod Manx got into the seat behind Thelma and closed the door.

"No, he's around here somewhere. I haven't seen him today. When I saw him yesterday he was sober. He didn't say anything about going anywhere. Did you ask Heather?" I nodded. "Well, I'm not surprised she didn't know. He'll turn up."

As Ringo started the engine, I heard a bellow of rage from the side of the house and a stocky man with a fringe of gray curly hair and a very red face came reeling into view, yelling at the top of his lungs, "Thelma! Wait, come back!"

It was Wolf Lambert. He had been tipsy and rather charming when I met him before. Today he looked blind drunk—angry and out of control.

The black SUV drove off. There was no sign that they had heard Wolf, and now they were leaving him and me in a cloud of dust.

I couldn't blame them. I wasn't very happy about being anywhere near Wolf at this point. Worse yet, he was between me and my car, weaving his way forward, as if to meet me halfway.

I detoured toward the front door of the tasting room, thinking to get help, but Wolf cut me off. He was moving faster than I had expected, with an unsettling drunken cunning. The voice of the BMW driver carried through the window, explaining to his friends and Heather how the bite of tannin in the Pinot Noir made it a good investment for aging.

Wolf was between me and the winery door. I made a wide circle around toward the other side of the building where the wine barrels were stacked. Maybe I could get behind the stack and he would forget I was there. The way he was staggering, maybe he would trip.

Wolf followed, and when he saw me behind the stacked barrels, he laughed and grabbed hold of the barrel on the end, as if to yank it out of the way. That wasn't too bright, considering that if the barrels fell out of formation, they would roll out between us and hinder his progress.

"Don't you girls touch those sweet wines till we try the robust reds," the BMW driver warned from inside the tasting room.

This was silly. Wolf seemed almost too drunk to stand. The people were just a few feet away. Something about his vacant eyes worried me enough that I hesitated to leave the safety of the chest-high rows of barrels, but I wasn't quite scared enough to call for help—yet.

Wolf staggered and caught himself on the full-sized barrel at the end of his side of the row. I hesitated, waiting to see which way he would go. He smiled, his red face lit with a kind of foggy cunning, and worked his way along the stack, leaning heavily on it for support. As he rounded the corner, I headed back toward the parking lot in front of the tasting room. This could work.

Wolf was panting now. He pulled himself around the end of the row, as if uncertain what to hang onto. He overbalanced and the row of barrels tilted and collapsed. Wrenched out of whatever had been holding them in balance, the first row started to roll out of formation. Wolf went down with a sudden yelp.

I hugged the corner of the building as the barrels rolled away toward the far reaches of the parking lot, but the second row never budged. I cautiously proceeded around the edge. If Wolf seemed unhurt, I intended to make my escape. But as I rounded the stack, with the first row gone, I could see one of the barrels in the second row was not empty.

I walked around past Wolf, who was lying, too stunned to move, on the ground. No one inside the winery appeared to have been disturbed by the rolling barrels outside. Through the open window the BMW driver directed his friends' attention to "overtones of bell pepper."

I stared into the open top of the end barrel in the second row. The first row had hidden it, but a pair of legs in blue jeans, with feet wearing expensive new running shoes were sticking out of the barrel's open head. The white soles of the shoes were stained green as if he had been walking on a green lawn. Bending down to look, I could see the top of a man's head pressed to his knees, his elbows bent, hands pressed together in a parody of prayer. He had been stuffed, backside first into the barrel. The back of his neck, with short brown hair, was also visible and I could just see the sunken red line of a ligature mark around his neck. He must have been folded up into a jackknife position to be stuffed in there. I didn't have to touch the rigid body. Its absolute stillness proclaimed its death.

Through the open window the BMW driver's voice floated out, "Not enough body for a Cabernet."

"Way too much body in this barrel out here," I said with a sigh.

An incoherent shout behind me reminded me to check on Wolf Lambert. The fall had stunned him. His breathing was short, and he stared into the middle distance, muttering something I couldn't understand at all—when he fell off the wagon, he fell pretty far.

Looking at his red face, I suddenly remembered what Thelma had said about Wolf taking Antabuse. If he had gotten this drunk with that drug in his system he might be well on his way to joining the anonymous party in the barrel.

I pulled my cell phone out of my purse, called 911, and explained Wolf's medical problem. Then I hesitantly added that it looked as if there might be someone in even worse shape, lodged in an inaccessible place. I didn't say there was a "deceased person stuffed in a wine barrel"— though there wasn't much doubt in my mind. I crouched down by Wolf, who was panting incoherently and muttering "Thelma" from time to time. I was worried that he was going to stop breathing.

The Baronsville police car didn't take long to arrive with sirens blaring. This brought the wine-tasting patrons out to see what the commotion was. It wasn't till they walked out of the tasting room that I realized I hadn't even thought to ask them if they could help. They didn't look too useful. Their concern about Wolf's health problems was tempered with a strong dose of irritation that their wine country afternoon was going to be interrupted. The BMW driver immediately went to check his car to be sure that the rolling barrels and emergency vehicles were not endangering it.

A fire truck followed the police car, and soon after a paramedic team arrived. I told them I had heard Wolf might be on Antabuse, and they started to give him oxygen and some kind of intravenous drip. While the paramedics surrounded Wolf, the policeman walked me away from the barrels. I explained how Wolf had knocked the first row over, revealing the body. He listened impassively and went over to look at the body in the barrel without touching it. Then he went to use the radio in his car.

A highly skeptical Baronsville police chief arrived soon after. There was a wistful look in his eyes as he questioned me, as if hoping to discover I had smuggled the body in my trunk from the big evil city and concealed it on the property simply for the purpose of causing trouble for the honest citizens of Baronsville. When I described the gray Jaguar I had seen on the property, he grew silent. His younger deputy blurted out, "That sounds like Carlo Baron's car. He shares a frontage road with this property—it used to be all one winery thirty years back."

His superior's glare silenced him.

The worst part about the next few hours was explaining to Mulligan why I was sure I could not get there in time for dinner.

He was silent for several seconds and then he said, "I'll be there as soon as I can. By the way, where the hell are you?"

"I'm in Baronsville, it's about an hour and a half north of the Golden Gate Bridge, but Mulligan, what about your conference?"

"Most of it is over. I was going to dedicate the rest of my weekend to debauchery, anyway. It would work a lot better if you were there."

"My, you do know how to turn a girl's head. But what about Yogi and Boo Boo?"

"Who?"

"Your army buddies. Sorry, I forgot their names."

"They can fend for themselves. Why? Did you want me to bring them?"

"No, thank you."

"You think I'm joking. But never mind. Harvey and Wally are very good in this type of situation. I'll tell them where I'm going just in case we vanish into the wilderness."

"Mulligan, it's Sonoma County, not Antarctica." I regretted that as soon as it was out of my mouth. "Joking." I said into the brief silence.

"I'm guessing you've had a pretty rough afternoon. I'll see you in an hour or so."

The county sheriff now approached and waited politely for me to finish, so I gave Mulligan quick directions and finished the call.

Then I explained again to the sheriff everything I had seen. He nodded impatiently through the Jaguar part of it and asked several questions about Thelma, Rod, and Ringo. I omitted what kind of business they had with Wolf, but he seemed to know about that already, from the grim set of his mouth and the way he was looking around the property as if expecting to see unsavory activities behind every bush. He got my cell phone number and I gave him the address from the brochure of the cottage where Ambrose had reserved a room. At that point the sheriff was happy to send me on my way. They knew how to treat tourists. The two couples in the BMW had already been dispatched with alacrity as soon as the sheriff discovered they hadn't seen anything useful.

I told the sheriff that my friend was driving up from San Francisco to meet me at this address. He conferred with the Baronsville chief of police. There appeared to be some questions about jurisdiction, but it was the sheriff who told me I could take my car and wait for Mulligan at the front gate. While I was waiting I called the Valley of the Moon Cottage and told them I would be checking in after dinner. They had a couple of recommendations of places nearby. Mulligan could do what he wanted, I was not driving back to San Francisco at this point.

Mulligan arrived just as the county coroner's van was leaving. Wolf had long ago been transported to the nearest hospital.

Mulligan parked his car and came over and hugged me. "Are you okay?"

"Yeah. I still don't know whose body it was in the wine barrel."

"Now tell me again what you were doing here?"

"I got this letter—look could we talk about this over dinner, I am starving and they said I could go."

"Okay." Mulligan looked a little puzzled. "I guess there are some places to eat near here."

"Ambrose offered me his reservations at a cottage over in the Valley of the Moon. When I called to tell them I'd be a little late they told me about a restaurant nearby."

Mulligan blinked at me, "Should I feel ambushed?"

"Only if you want to be."

We drove over, each in our own rental car. The Valley Pioneer Ovens was a shabby-looking rock building with historical plaques in prominent places in the parking lot and on the doors. The interior was surprisingly comfortable and immaculate, with scrubbed thick rock walls, hung with local artists' paintings of vineyards and foothills. The floor was plain wood, the tablecloths sumptuous and white. The handwritten menu featured a wood-burning pizza oven and local wines.

"I'll pay for dinner," Mulligan said with a smile. "I am

saving the money I would have spent buying steaks and drinks for Harvey and Wally."

I felt suddenly shy and we both sipped wine, buttered bread, and put aside the question of cottage in the Valley of the Moon.

"Sorry you're missing your buddies and your evening events."

"It's okay."

We talked about the menu, the town, and the traffic on the drive up from San Francisco. We both ordered pasta, comfort food, which the restaurant did well.

After we had eaten, I took a deep breath and jumped in. "I may be insane to ask you to this cottage I'm staying in, but it would be a shame to waste it on one person—it has a hot tub and everything. So crazy or not, I'm inviting you."

"Well, up till now, you did seem sane. If occasionally stubborn and always opinionated. But I like that in a woman." Now he was smiling. Sitting across the table from him made me a little giddy.

"I just get curious about things."

"Haven't you ever heard what happened to curious cats?"

"Sure. Curiosity filled the cat." I was smiling at him in a way that had nothing to do with the joke. "That has to be true. I saw it on a postcard today in downtown San Francisco."

He smiled back. "Well if you saw it on a postcard, then it must be true. What am I going to do with you?"

"I was wondering that myself."

He leaned across the table and like a spark leaping from one electrical connection to another we drew close and kissed. "I did have a few ideas, but just between us, let me settle up and you can lead the way back to that cottage."

"Yes," I said with a sigh.

A Ton of Trouble

The address I'd been given was off Adobe Canyon Road up a winding side road shaded by enough trees to intensify the growing dusk. We pulled into the tiny parking area where a farmhouse sat, and a sign with a spotlight on it read "Valley of the Moon Cottage—by appointment only, ring bell." A thin man in his forties with graying blond hair and toothbrush mustache answered the door, said he'd been expecting us, and invited us into a small foyer where a desk with a guest book and a stack of brochures served as a check-in counter.

I presented him with the reservation information Ambrose had given me and he checked us in, telling us to leave our cars where we parked them.

"It's a few yards to the cottage from here," he said. His quiet voice had a relaxing effect on me. I realized that I was operating on a city wavelength still—expecting him to raise a fuss about accommodating a second car. Mulligan stood back and let me arrange everything until the owner asked if we needed help with the luggage. Mulligan said he could carry both our bags and the man waited while he extracted them from our cars. Then he led us behind the farmhouse and across a rustic bridge. "There's a creek on the property," he pointed out. "You'll see it in the morning—there's a nice marked path alongside it that goes up into the hills if you feel like a stroll and Sugarloaf Ridge State Park is just up the road if you feel like serious recreation." He cleared his throat, looking from Mulligan to me and back. "The hot tub is on a private deck under the stars. There are towels and robes on the vanity next to the door."

He let us into the cottage and turned on the lights, which were soft and indirect, and bid us good night. It was so quiet that we could hear him as he walked back across the bridge.

Mulligan and I looked around the cottage. A dozen roses

stood in a ceramic vase on a table, next to a basket of fruit and two glasses, a small stand held a bucket of ice and a bottle of champagne. At the other end of the cottage through an archway a rose-colored lamp over the king-sized bed was visible. Opposite the table with the fruit and roses, a tiny iron fireplace was set in a corner between two large windows. Lace curtains and the growing darkness outside hid any view.

W ant me to start a fire?" Mulligan asked.

I sat on the loveseat and looked at the fireplace. It had cooled down as it got dark. "If you want. I'm not cold."

"It's all set up. Looks like I just need to light a match." He crouched a few feet away and I examined his back with great interest. Somehow it was more comforting than the rest of the room, with its flowers, bed with rose-colored bedspread and the hot tub steaming on the deck just beyond the sliding door.

The fire began to blaze and Mulligan stood up, dusting his knees, though the place was immaculate. "Would you like some champagne?" he asked, meeting my eyes for the briefest moment.

"Please."

He brought the bottle along with the glasses and we settled down to sip champagne and watch the fire. "Tell me again how you know this pornographer slash wine maker."

"He directed the Hanged Man films, I met him at Francesca Benedict's funeral and came down to his winery a few days later to ask him about her."

"He directed the Hanged Man films? That sounds vaguely familiar."

"They were sort of based on the Tarot card, the Hanged Man—about a man who survives execution and goes around getting revenge. They turned into slasher films—there were about a dozen of them and he retired on the profits. Anyway, I met him at Francesca Benedict's funeral and came down to his winery a few days later to ask him about her."

"I remember that trip. I took care of the cat, just like I'll be doing next week while you're here in the Bay Area." His face was solemn.

"Um, well," his guarded expression was making me nervous. "I met Wolf twice before. Once in Seattle and again when I visited his winery. The person I really liked was Thelma, his bookkeeper."

"Who also starred in his X-rated films."

"Right. But now she's making her own. In fact, she invited me to the set where they're filming tomorrow."

"What?" He stared at me and shook his head. "We're just started getting together and now you want to visit some kind of porn film set—wouldn't you like to wait till the bloom is off the rose a little and we get jaded?"

I took a deep breath and involuntarily glanced over at the dozen roses—it was easier than looking at the bed.

I took another deep breath. "So you're saying you expect us to get jaded?"

"I hadn't been—no. But why start with all that sleazy stuff?"

"Excuse me," I tapped his arm in mock irritation, mainly an excuse to touch him. "I don't know if we've exactly started or not, it's hard to tell. But I haven't seen anything sleazy about anything we've done. Anyway, it isn't the pornography that interests me—okay, that's a little titillating. I've only seen one of those films—really part of one. I walked out on it half-way through."

"So far your explanation is making things even less clear."

Just as clear as my head was, with the wine and now champagne. I sighed. "If it was just a regular porn shoot I wouldn't be interested. But because it's plus-sized women, and someone I know, I'm interested. Then there's the movie part. No one's ever offered to let me see any kind of movie set. My plan is to leave before the porn part."

"I've seen a few of these things, Jo, and there's nothing left once you take out the sex. If it makes you feel squeamish from the beginning, why even bother to go?"

"Because I'm curious and I like Thelma." I realized I hadn't mentioned the strange amends letter, but it didn't seem like a time to complicate things with Wolf's adventures in sobriety.

Mulligan sighed. "It's hard to keep up with you. This is the woman you told me about, who was trying to get you to strip down and jump into a hot tub for some kind of three-way arrangement with this jaded old film director."

"That's the one! Hmm, I forgot that I mentioned that."

"It must have been the wine. You brought back a very nice burgundy as I recall. Was that from this guy's winery?"

"No." For some reason I shivered a little, the thought of wine brought back the image of the body in the barrel. Mulligan moved closer. The fire was warm, but he was much warmer. He may have misinterpreted the shiver, but being closer to him did help. I sighed again. "I went to a different winery for that wine. They weren't open—I didn't want to— anyway, that wasn't from Lambert's winery."

Mulligan shook his head and looked down at me with mild

exasperation, although there was a faint gleam of amusement underneath it all.

"Thelma said you could come," I ventured.

Mulligan smiled. "Do we have to perform?"

"Of course not!" I left out Thelma's invitation to jump in if the spirit moved.

"And you wonder why I'm beginning to question your judgment."

"You're saying my judgment hasn't been the best?"

He slipped his arm around my shoulder and pulled me close. "Would you like to continue this conversation over in roseland?" He indicated the pink-lit bed.

"We could turn off the lamp, if you don't like pink."

"Some kinds of pink I'm quite fond of." He muttered into my ear.

With his body pressed along the length of mine, I found myself lapsing into incoherence.

Holding each other tightly, exploring each other breathlessly, neither of us spoke much for a long time.

It may have been wrong, or too soon, but it felt right and inevitable. We slipped into a haze of pleasure. Eventually, we did move to the king-sized bed that dominated the bedroom.

Much later, thoroughly exhausted and drowsy, we lay resting in each other's arms, Mulligan asked, "Do you still want to see dirty movies?"

"Not right now. But ask me after you've gone back to Seattle and I'm here alone for a couple of weeks."

"You are incorrigible."

"We never got to the hot tub," I reminded him.

"Do you mind?"

"No. I'm good."

A little later when I thought he was asleep, he opened his

eyes and said solemnly, "If you insist on going to this thing tomorrow, I'll go with you. I don't want you going alone."

"You think it's not safe?"

"I think there's some question about that, yeah."

"And maybe you're a little curious yourself."

"Get some sleep and we'll deal with that in the morning."

W e made it through the night with no major guilt attacks, and we even cuddled our way into a mind-shattering morning communion.

After the excellent coffee that came with the cabin we wandered into the morning sunlight. It was already warm outside. I had the hollowed-out light feeling that can only be produced by a night of passion. A bit stiff and sore, but in a good way.

I looked up at Mulligan and he just smiled and took my hand. We talked very little, as if words could destroy us. We took a walk along the creek before breakfast, stared at the small stream of water, and shared a kiss that was more affectionate than urgent.

We decided to drive over to Baronsville for a proper breakfast. The town square was bordered with two-story buildings with high narrow windows, built of rock cut from local quarries. I felt a certain distant sorrow for the anonymous body in the barrel. We bought a local newspaper with a huge headline reading EXTRA—BARON SON-IN-LAW MURDERED. In the small café where we ate, almost every other customer had a copy of the paper.

The article identified the body as Steve Farquar, son-in-law of the local landowner whose grandfather had founded the town. Farquar had worked for the Baronsville property management company owned by his father-in-law. The police had stated that the cause of death was still unknown, but the way that the body was found suggested a homicide. The article also mentioned that the owner of the property had been hospitalized for a possible toxic reaction. That made it sound as if Wolf's winery had been under a chemical cloud, but he had bigger problems right now than whether his wine sales would suffer.

Mulligan called his old army buddies at breakfast. Eavesdropping on his end of the conversation, I learned that they were agreeing to get together at the next convention.

"I've got to get back to San Francisco to get my stuff from the hotel," Mulligan said. "I'll call for a late checkout, but there's only so much time." I was in a good enough mood myself that I might even have given up the idea of visiting Thelma's film set if he had suggested going back to the room for a soak in the hot tub. He was entitled to some time to recuperate. Maybe he was a little curious, too.

The address Thelma had given me proved to be a large house, in the foothills on the outskirts of Baronsville, where a few housing developments were crowding out the cattle pastures. A block of other large houses ringed the cul-de-sac tucked into small thickets of bushes. Several cars were parked along the block, including the hulking black SUV the Manx brothers drove.

We were greeted at the door by a stunningly beautiful African American woman. She was short with an elaborate braided and beaded hairstyle, wearing a brightly flowered sarong that clung to a figure that was spectacular on a large scale, although she was closer to my size than Thelma's. She introduced herself as Suzy. She was showing a great deal of café au lait cleavage through the top of the sarong. When she moved, it was apparent that it was also slit up the side to the hip. She giggled when she saw that neither Mulligan nor I could help but stare. She moved the flowered fabric slightly to show high-cut red silk panties through the slit. Then she threw back her head and laughed when we both blinked.

The living room she led us into was spacious—the fireplace looked as if it could roast an ox. What must have been the room's usual furniture, a sofa and a couple of armchairs, were pushed back to the walls and a bed had been set up a short distance from the fireplace.

A stocky young man wearing a camouflage jacket and pants looked up from the sofa, where he had spread out an assortment of lenses. He didn't look old enough to buy a ticket to an adult film, let alone photograph one. He was chatting with a thin woman in her early thirties who was rolling a floodlight on a wheeled platform into position around the bed and fireplace area, where several other lights had been set up on tripods. Her hair was shaved into complex patterns that must be next season's hottest fashion, and she wore a black T-shirt, jeans, and thick-soled leather shoes.

Thelma made a dramatic entrance in a purple silk gown with her ample middle cinched in improbably, and an Elizabethan style ruff around her neck, which did not interfere with the exposure of most of her very impressive breasts. Her bright red hair spilled down her back in a complicated arrangement. A large-sized blonde with an elaborate hairstyle followed Thelma with a small comb and a can of hairspray and made a few last-minute touch-ups. "I'm so glad you could come, Jo!" Thelma called out. Turning to the blonde, she said, "Let me introduce our makeup woman, and future video star—"

"Thelma!" Rod Manx came in from a back room down the hall dressed only in bikini underpants. Immediately on his heels was a tiny middle-aged Asian woman wearing a black skirt, white polo shirt, and horn-rimmed glasses with a chain fastened to them to keep them from escaping. She was holding out a stack of Scottish tartan material.

Rod kept resolutely out of her reach. "I'm not wearing a skirt."

Thelma swept over to look up into Rod's eyes. "It's a kilt, Roddy, didn't you see *Braveheart*? It's very macho."

Ringo came in as she spoke. His sunglasses had red-tinted lenses today. He was shirtless and wearing blue jeans and was holding a bagpipe out at arm's length, as if it might bite him.

"It's very sexy, boys." Thelma's voice was earnest, but there was a hint of embarrassment at the rebellion of the troops. Maybe being the director and the star of this type of film in particular made discipline a bit more difficult. "See, that's one of the ways I think we can get more women interested. Women are crazy to see what's under a Scotsman's kilt."

"That doesn't explain where this comes in," Ringo said, still standing in the doorway and looking darkly at the bagpipe.

"Wait till we get going, baby, you'll be surprised!" Thelma said with a wicked chuckle.

Mulligan and I exchanged glances. I had seen previews of this side of her, he hadn't.

"Okay, okay, just so you don't expect me to play it," Ringo grumbled, taking a kilt out of the Asian woman's hands and turning back to where he had come.

His brother took the remaining kilt and followed him, "I

told you she's going to lose her money on this one," Rod muttered in a tone that didn't sound as if he cared whether or not he was heard.

I turned back to Thelma, who had regained whatever composure she might have lost at her stars' rebellion. "Wow, what a gorgeous costume," I said.

"Wonderful, isn't it?" Thelma twirled slowly to show off the skirt. "Hiromi, who sewed it, makes Ren Faire clothes, and this is a sort of Scottish castle fantasy scene. The bodice here has Velcro so that those boys can rip it off when they light my fire." She demonstrated, pulling a few inches of Velcro loose.

"Stop that!" The small Asian woman shrieked. Everyone in the room blinked.

"Hiromi's right. You'll fall right out of that, if you open it up too early Thelma," the blonde with the hairspray scolded. "Wait until the camera's running to show your goodies—I had enough trouble packing you into that, I don't want to have to do it more times than I need to today."

Thelma laughed and so did the technicians. Even Mulligan smiled—although Hiromi bustled back out of the room, trailing wisps of tartan cloth.

I introduced Mulligan to Thelma.

"This is a great house," he said.

"It's Herb's." Thelma smiled and gestured at the elegant living room. "He's got several, and he's going to let us use them."

"Is Herb here today?" I looked around.

She giggled. "Oh, no. Herb doesn't like girls, although he is an F.A."

"Fat admirer," I helpfully translated to Mulligan, who nodded absently, his eyes drawn to Suzy, who had gone off to a corner and was now limbering up with some stretching exercises that tested the limits of the split in the sarong.

"Herb shows up when they film guy-on-guy videos for the bear market," Thelma said with an irrepressible giggle.

"Bear market as opposed to bull market?" I had to ask.

Now Thelma laughed heartily. "No honey, bears are big gay men, and the men who like them are sometimes called chubby chasers—you've heard that term."

"Yeah," Mulligan spoke up. He didn't sound amused.

"The bear films are different from what I'm doing—wall-to-wall action and not much plot. Sometimes the opposite sex is so opposite." She giggled. "I want to do films that appeal to women, that's why I thought of this Scottish scene—it's so romantic." She gestured to Suzy, who had moved over to chat with the cameraman. "Then Suzy is going to play the sarong-clad island girl, and we have shorts and a pith helmet for the guy who is working with her. Women like to see a little leg even before the shorts come off. That guy's not here yet—we'll do his scene later today, but we should start filming this scene soon."

I looked at where all the lights and cameras were focused—around the bed and fireplace. Along another wall out of camera range, a card table held an array of chips, dip, soft drinks, and small bottles of water. A coffee table next to it had been furnished with a workmanlike array of vibrators and dildos. A giant-sized jar that had once held peanut butter was now full of condoms. Next to it were a couple of king-sized pump bottles of lubricant and several packets of piña colada mix.

"What's that for?" I pointed to the most innocent looking item.

The woman in the black T-shirt, who was threading an

electric cord around the feet of the table, looked over to see what I was pointing at. "Oh, the piña colada mix. That's our secret weapon."

Everyone in earshot laughed uproariously, although Mulligan and I were mystified. No one explained further. I guess it really was a secret.

"So you and Wolf are still on good terms," I said to Thelma.

"Oh, yes. When I told him I wasn't filming a money shot he said I was crazy, so we're doing it. But he thinks I'm going to fail and come crawling back." Thelma smiled. "I don't think so. But I'm keeping my kneepads handy just in case he's right." She clapped her hands and whistled loudly. "Okay, let's get set up and get down to it." I blinked in surprise. She turned to us. "If you want, you can sit on the sofa and watch."

"We hate to miss it, but we've got to get going. I've got a flight to catch." Mulligan took my arm, nodded at Thelma, and began to pull us toward the door.

"Thanks for inviting us." Now I wanted to leave, but I hated to offend her.

"I'm sorry you can't stay," Thelma said, following us to the door and seeming a little hurt.

We got to the door when a heavy knock sounded.

"Baronsville Police."

I looked over my shoulder. Suzy whispered something to Thelma, but I didn't catch it. She turned and made her slow progress back to what must have been a bedroom or changing area.

I looked at Mulligan. "I guess there's no chance that could be Harvey and Wally."

He sighed. "No."

The knocking came again. No one moved to answer the door. "We should open it," I said. Suzy nodded, obviously having seen a few episodes of "Cops."

I opened the door and a man and a woman in police uniform stood on the doorstep. "We were told we could find Mandy Hanson here," the man said.

I turned back to Suzy. "We're just visiting."

"Mandy Hanson is Thelma's real name," Suzy confided. "She's in back . . ."

"May we come in?"

"Uh, I guess so," Suzy said. We all stood aside.

I backed up and so did Mulligan, keeping hold of my arm. Much as we both now wanted to leave, this was not the time. We all went back into the living room, with its bed and lighting.

The police officers took in the room, the pushed-back furniture, table full of sex toys, and the lights trained on the bed. The man with the video camera had prudently disappeared out the back while we were debating, but the woman setting up the lights simply stopped, sat back on her heels next to the light she had been adjusting, and waited.

"Home movies?" One of the cops said.

"Yes, we were," Thelma came out of the back wearing a

crisp cotton sundress. She had peeled off that elaborate getup in record time—score one for Velcro. The sundress effect was somewhat marred by her heavy makeup, elaborate hairstyle, and the supermarket flip-flop sandals on her feet. "We're filming an adult video. This is private property. Perfectly legal."

"It is if you've got a permit to film. Are you Mandy Hanson?"

"Yes, I am."

"I'm sorry if we've come at a bad time, ma'am, but we need to talk to you about the murder of Steve Farquar. Could you come with us for a formal interview?"

We all stood thunderstruck while the two officers moved to flank Thelma/Mandy as if she might try to escape.

"Look, officers, these technical people are all on the clock. Could we do this interview tomorrow, or do I need to be calling my lawyer?"

It was a moment before I realized that the cameraman had come back into the room, surreptitiously raised his camera, and begun filming.

The police officers didn't seem upset by the idea that a day's worth of adult films would be lost. "I'm afraid we'll have to insist." We all followed them out to the street where the police car was parked. Mulligan let go of my arm and we found ourselves standing on the sidewalk.

We all followed them out to the curb. "Am I under arrest?" Thelma asked in a small voice.

"Not at this point, ma'am. But we'd like to talk to you down at the Baronsville Police Station. It's down on Fourth and Main."

Thelma turned her head, "Suzy, can you call a lawyer and meet us there?"

"I'll be there. But Thelma, the only lawyer I know is my tax attorney."

"Call Bud Harkness, he's in the book."

They had reached the squad car, and it took several moments to maneuver Thelma into the backseat.

Suzy, the video cameraman, the woman in the black T-shirt who was setting up lights, the Asian wardrobe mistress, and the blond makeup woman all stood on the curb. Something was missing from this picture.

"Where are those guys in kilts?" I whispered to Mulligan, as the police car drove away.

Mulligan shrugged.

"Excuse me, I just want to look and see." I went around to the side of the house and looked through the backyard. Sure enough there was an alley and I could see the big black sport-utility vehicle with Ringo sitting behind the wheel. The engine was idling. I went toward it, the SUV started to drive away down the alley. I tracked its progress on the other side of the tall fence as I walked around the side of the house. As I arrived in the front yard, the SUV had just made a soft left turn and was driving at a moderate clip in the opposite direction from the patrol car. The cameraman had stopped shooting. I went up to him and said, "Why don't you shoot those guys leaving in the SUV?" I pointed.

He shook his head, "They're too far off. I couldn't pick up much at this distance." He turned and followed Suzy and the makeup woman into the house.

I went back to Mulligan, who was still standing on the walkway. "So much for the Manx brothers."

He stared at me. "The what?"

"The guys in kilts. Their name is Manx—their nom de porn."

He nodded. "Okay."

"They left."

"Okay. Where shall we have lunch?"

We stopped at a little delicatessen on the town square, across from the Sonoma Mission, and bought sandwiches to take back to the cottage. Once there, we sat down with a glass of wine apiece to stare at the view. Eating the sandwiches had replaced hunger with a vague knot of dread.

"This is too weird for me, Jo. What did you expect would happen when you took me there?"

"I thought it would be fun, sexy, maybe borderline shocking. Oh, I don't know! Obviously, I didn't expect the police. Sorry. I'm sorry I'm not Nina. I wish she were alive. I wish I didn't have whatever this thing is I have for you. Maybe it's wrong."

I looked away. That was about as much apologizing as I could muster. I couldn't tell if I was angry or close to tears.

"I know who you are, Jo, and I care about you. It just seems like since Nina died, things have been getting crazier. I miss the way that she could make me feel that everything was okay."

"I miss that, too. I sure can't do it for anyone, even myself."

"No one can make everything okay anymore."

"And you're saying everything is not okay?" The minute I said it I wanted to take it back.

He paused, but had the good grace not to roll his eyes. Instead he hugged me and I hugged him back. "My flight is at 5:00 and I've got to check out and get my stuff from the hotel."

"I'll be back next week or the week after," was all I said. "I'll let you know as soon as I know how long it will be."

"Call and give me the number where you're staying."

"I'll do that. But you can call on my cell phone any time.

"Okay." We kissed deeply and pulled away reluctantly. He got into the car and then rolled down the window.

"Jo?"

"Yes."

"Nothing. Just take care."

"You, too. Call when you get back to Seattle."

I kissed him again through the driver's side window and watched as he drove off and left me standing in the parking lot across the bridge from the cottage, uncomforted by the view. I went and sat in the small garden that surrounded the cottage. But I was too distracted to be soothed by the rustic setting. With a regretful look at the hot tub, I checked out of the cottage, got in the rental car, and headed for San Francisco. The manager suggested the Black Point cutoff to Novato to avoid the traffic around Santa Rosa. As I drove, I wondered if Mulligan, who had missed that information, had managed to clear the Golden Gate Bridge without getting stuck in a flood of people coming back into the City to prepare for their workweek.

Finally, I got across the bridge and reached the Marina turnoff. I headed south toward Nob Hill and Mrs. Madrone's corporate condo on Pine Street, feeling as if I were heading for the school principal's office.

12

I checked in with the security guard in the lobby to let him to know my car would be in the parking garage. I went in and straight up to the suite, where my garment bag and suitcase were still sitting just inside the door, still unpacked.

I ignored them and took the folder Ambrose had given me off the table and sat down. But I didn't look at it for a while. I just sat with the open folder and tried to absorb the events of the last two days. They didn't sink in very readily.

Reluctantly, I turned to the folder to see where I would be going tomorrow. There were three addresses in San Francisco for offices of A Friend in Need, women's health and legal projects, for me to visit. My usual tactic was to read some background on each one and decide on an approach. Sometimes I would walk in as if I needed services—more often I would stop by and ask about volunteer opportunities. At the moment I couldn't seem to quite focus enough to come up with an idea.

I stowed the folder in my briefcase and was just about to think about where I might get some dinner, or at least a latte to jump-start my thought processes, when my cell phone rang.

"This is Sedona Yamada from the Bud Harkness firm, I left a message earlier."

"Sorry, I just got back to my hotel. I haven't retrieved messages yet. The name Harkness is familiar. Is this about Thelma or Mandy or whatever her name is?"

"Yes. Thelma is an old friend of Mr. Harkness and he asked me to represent her. I understand you were there in Baronsville a few hours ago when the police took her in?"

"That's right."

"You were at Lambert's Lair Winery when the body was found yesterday, too, weren't you?"

"Um," I suddenly wondered if the woman I was talking to was really who she said. "Look, Ms.—what did you say your name was?"

"Yamada. I got your number from Thelma. I'm not a reporter. But I can understand how you might be concerned. Would you feel better if I gave you a reference and you checked me out and called me back? I'm actually in San Francisco also at the moment. Here, let me give you a number to call."

"Whose number?"

"Ambrose Terrell. He works for Mrs. Madrone and he can verify my number."

I was too startled to say anything. But I took down Ambrose's number, which I already had, said I'd call her back, and then I called Ambrose. I got his answering machine, but before I could finish the message he picked up the phone. There was classical music playing in the background.

Ambrose sighed, "Aren't you supposed to be finishing off a relaxing weekend?"

"It was a really wonderful cottage, Ambrose, thank you for the reservation, but Mulligan had to leave this afternoon, so I came back. I'm sorry you missed the opportunity to get up there with your friend."

"Oh, there will be other weekends. I share a flat with him when I'm in the City, so when he gets back he'll be able to take me to the opera and apologize properly for leaving me to my own devices here."

"I would have waited till tomorrow to call," I said, "but I found a dead body over the weekend."

"Surely you're joking."

"No." I sighed. "I wish I were. The best thing I can tell you about this situation is that I'm not personally involved."

"And yet, you're calling me on a Sunday evening."

"Someone gave me your number as a reference. Are you acquainted with Sedona Yamada from the Bud Harkness firm?"

"Not personally, but the name is familiar. Hang on a sec." I envisioned Ambrose checking a massive database on his computer, but it might have been a Rolodex. "Yes. I have her listed as a board member of some women's nonprofit groups that we've given grants to," he said. "Nothing major. Harkness is major. He's a big time antitrust lawyer, lots of Democratic Party and charitable connections there. He lives in Sonoma County, coincidentally. You didn't offend him—or her—did you, Jo?"

"Nothing like that. I just want to double-check that this is Ms. Yamada. She says she's representing a woman who may be implicated in a murder in Sonoma over the weekend."

There was a moment of silence. "So its not just a dead body, it's a murder? You went up to Sonoma for a nice, hot weekend to melt down those Mulligan inhibitions—you did do that, didn't you?"

"Um, yes."

"So where does the murder come in?"

"Can I tell you tomorrow?"

"I am so glad Mrs. Madrone is out of the country. Try not to do anything rash this evening. Where are you, now?"

"I'm back on Pine Street."

"All right. How about dinner tomorrow?"

He suggested a restaurant one block up and a few blocks east on Bush Street, and we agreed to meet there the next evening.

I called Sedona Yamada back. She answered on the first ring. "So do I pass muster?"

"Ambrose Terrell seems to think you're legitimate and he doesn't make mistakes about much."

"So we can talk about the murder?"

"Ms. Yamada—"

"Call me Sedona."

"Sedona then. I did find that man's body in the wine barrel at Lambert's Lair Winery. But all I saw was the top of his head. The next day I saw in the paper that he was a relative of the guy the town was named after. Who was the victim exactly?"

"His name was Steve Farquar. He was married to Carlo Baron's daughter and worked for the Baronsville Realty Company. Being a very wealthy man, and a major local landowner, the father-in-law has clout."

"And they think Thelma did it?"

She sighed. "They didn't arrest her, mainly because of some other things that have turned up that I can't talk about right now. The whole thing is just starting to look a little more complicated than they thought at first."

"How is Thelma?"

"She's hanging in there. The police suspect her, but so far they don't have enough evidence to arrest her. Thelma is a small business owner in the community, and they don't have

an open-and-shut case. But in the meantime she's under a
cloud of suspicion, and it's not great for her accounting business."

"Wouldn't making adult films be dangerous to begin with,
if she were worried about the Chamber of Commerce?"

There was a pause and I could almost hear Sedona Yamada silently sigh. "A person's private life, or even an adult
video business is one thing, Ms. Fuller. A murder accusation
is quite another. I'd like to have the rest of this conversation
in person, if you don't mind. I spoke to Thelma this afternoon
and there was something she asked me to tell you. It's not
something that I can say over the telephone. Can you spare
me some time tomorrow?"

"Okay, would you like to meet for coffee tomorrow morning?"

"If we can make it at eleven-thirty? I have to be in court
earlier, but I should be done before eleven."

"Well, I have to be at—" I looked at the address of the
first organization on my list. "It's at Tenth and Howard."

"Are you driving?"

"Is parking a problem?"

"Parking is always a problem in San Francisco—except
in the movies. If you'd like, I can pick you up there at
eleven—call if you're done sooner." She gave me her cell
phone number. "We can have lunch and I can drop you off
afterward or you can get a bus or a cab. That part of South of
Market is an urban neighborhood. Bring your street smarts."

S he was right about the neighborhood. The cab driver set me down between a store that sold restaurant equipment and an old office building, its doorway chained, barred, and padlocked with an "Enter on 10th Street" sign over the doors. Across the street a couple of men lounged in the sunshine smoking cigarettes in front of the faded turquoise awning of a seedy hotel.

The Friend in Need Center had a sliding metal gate in front of its storefront window, which had been pulled back just far enough to allow the glass door to open and shut, but I had to ring a bell and announce myself to a hard-eyed, gray-haired woman at a desk inside the door. She buzzed me in.

The brief description Ambrose had given me from the grant request represented that the place offered a full range of health services to women in need. Once in the door, I found myself in a room painted very bright yellow and decorated with children's crayon drawings. I suspected the yellow might get on my nerves very quickly. Something about one of the drawings caught my eye—red crayon blood spurting from a female figure being knifed by a man with a stethoscope. I looked at another child's drawing, small angels—well, they had wings—dripping azure crayon tears. What was this place?

Aside from the eagle-eyed, gray-haired woman there were two other women in the room. I almost thought "girls" as they seemed too young to be in high school—though they were probably teenagers, one blonde, one pale brunette, and definitely both very pregnant—sitting in molded plastic chairs that ringed a low table full of tired-looking magazines. The brunette, dressed in an inexpertly knitted green sweater and purple stirrup pants, was dozing quietly, while the blonde, in gray sweatshirt and sweatpants, stared at the magazines as if too tired to reach out and lift one. The woman in the sweats also wore house slippers. I wondered if they lived here. The woman behind the desk saw me looking at the teenagers and smiled briskly, like a surgeon happily picking up his scalpel.

"Were you referred by your health plan, or—how did you find out about us?"

"Um, you're in the Yellow Pages," I said with a shrug. "I should ask about the cost."

"There is never a fee, although we do accept donations and some of the health plans pay something if you have insurance. So, how far along are you?" she asked.

"What?" Her question took me by surprise, although my eyes flicked to the other two women, who didn't seem interested.

"Sit down. It's all right. Would you like some juice?"

I sat down. "No juice, thanks."

"Have you had an ultrasound? Because we can do that here. We can also do pregnancy tests here, if you're not sure. There's a nurse practitioner on duty." Her eyes flicked to the back. What else was there besides a nurse?

"Actually, I'm not sure." I stopped, because suddenly I

was sure. "Let me guess, the counseling you're offering doesn't include abortion as an option."

"We provide counseling. But you know in your heart that abortion can never be the answer."

"Okay, thanks. I just came in here to get some information."

"Of course, please feel free to come back. You don't want to make a mistake that will haunt you for the rest of your life." She got out some brochures, which I took without looking.

After my weekend with Mulligan, the general drift of her inquiry struck an unexpected nerve. I rose to go. "Would you like to give us your phone number, we can call and make sure you're okay?"

I shook my head, muttered something, and walked out, feeling I had somehow escaped from the twilight zone and stood outside on the sidewalk blinking at the brochures. The gory pictures confirmed that there was a definite agenda in the place I had just left. As I put the brochures into my purse, I saw that the woman inside the storefront was conferring with a platinum blond woman, who must have come from somewhere in the back. The blonde wore white denim pants and a pink angora sweater that looked as if it had been spun from fluffy bubble gum. Somehow I doubted that she was the nurse practitioner. She didn't seem to fit in with either the street or the storefront I had just come out of. Both women looked at me with unwelcoming expressions.

I moved down the block a bit and dialed Sedona Yamada's cell phone—it was a little after 10:00, but she answered immediately.

"You're in luck," she said. "I had a postponement on my morning hearing. I'm just getting into my car at the Hall of

Justice and I'm only a couple of blocks from you. Look for a red Honda Civic."

The blonde in the pink sweater came out of the storefront before I finished with the call. I stowed my cell phone away and started to scan the streets again. She stood several yards away while I waited, and she watched me with an expression that she might have thought was gentle concern, but it had a predatory edge to it that made me nervous.

A van pulled up with "Friend in Need" painted on the side of it, and the two pregnant women were escorted out of the storefront by their gray-haired guardian. They got into the van. The older woman said a few words to the driver, nodded to the blonde in the pink sweater, and used a ring of keys to let herself back into the center.

As the van drove off down the street, a small red car pulled up and lowered its passenger window, "Jo Fuller?"

"Sedona Yamada, I presume," I said. I took another look back at the blonde, who was now striding toward the car. "We had better take off. That very strange woman over there seems to be taking a keen interest in my situation."

"Probably the neighborhood watch committee."

"Well, she is taking down your license plate."

"Hey, I've worked for the Southern Poverty Law Center and the ACLU, I'm not easily intimidated," she said. "For all we know, she could be writing down the lyrics to a country western song that just came to her." She laughed, and I joined her, partly out of relief to be heading away from that strange place. I glanced back to see the blonde unlocking the door to go back again into the Friend in Need storefront.

Yamada was Japanese, short and plump, but I felt impossibly huge sitting on the seat next to her. She was in her early thirties and had a complicated but stylish haircut and auburn highlights.

She drove us about half a mile through more warehouses, factories, and condominiums with signs in front. "This used to be an industrial neighborhood, with a lot of working people living here," she said. "But the urban renewal thing has been chipping away at it. During the dot-com boom, a lot of Silicon Valley firms rented spaces, but the big force that's driving out small factories is the fact that some people can pay whatever the market will bear for housing. The city had some laws to protect artists who lived in their studios and the next thing they knew landlords were building these loft apartments and renting them as so-called live-work spaces for a fortune. Not too many poor people are left in this neighborhood and very few artists can afford to live here."

"Where do you live?"

"In the southern edge of Sonoma County—Petaluma."

When we got out of the car and walked along the sidewalk, I noticed she was half a foot shorter than my five foot eight. On a nondescript corner a block from a freeway overpass, with a charming view of a car wash, was the place she had chosen for lunch.

"Is it a bar?" I was curious.

"It's a funky, gay bar, but only at night." She smiled mischievously. "But they do good sandwiches and it's quiet in the daytime."

The place did lack the cigarette and sour humanity smell of a neighborhood bar. Light filtered in through large windows onto the scarred wooden tables along that wall and illuminated the bar across the room. There were no other customers. We sat at a table near the window and I idly watched a man vacuuming his car at the self-serve car wash. A businesslike Chinese woman gave us menus and brought chilled glasses of water with lemon slices.

Yamada would have looked out of place here if anyone had been around to notice. I was a little more in tune with the gritty warehouse district atmosphere in my poor-person-seeking-help outfit of plain olive green blouse and pants. She could have power lunched anywhere in town in her charcoal gray pinstriped skirt and blazer. Anchored with a stunning pearl pin, the iridescent scarf around her neck seemed green, gold, and then purple depending on how the light hit it. She must be doing well at the practice of law. We ordered tea and sandwiches.

She didn't even wait for the tea to brew. "I'm approaching you on Thelma's behalf to ask if there is any possibility we could get help from the Madrone Foundation for her defense."

"You mean to pay the lawyer fees?"

"Not exactly. Bud is donating my time pro bono—you know, as a good deed. It's the investigation where we need help. The Baronsville police are an excellent organization, but they seem to be concentrating on Thelma to the exclusion of other suspects. Possibly for local political reasons. Our hope is that you can find out who really killed this guy."

"You need a licensed private investigator."

"Do you think Mrs. Madrone would pay for one?"

"Hmm." I wasn't sure. "I'll ask her staff before I ask her. I still don't understand why Thelma is the main suspect. Did she know the murdered man at all?"

Sedona sighed, "She says she only spoke to him in passing when he came to talk to Wolf Lambert on business. Steve Farquar is married to the daughter of Carlo Baron, Lambert's next door neighbor. Mr. Baron is the grandson of the founder of Baronsville, and as the name would indicate he used to own it all at one time. It would be an understatement to say he's very entrenched in the area."

"It still doesn't sound like they have any reason to suspect Thelma."

"They may have an eyewitness that places her near the barrels the night Farquar was killed. The neighbor whose house sits on a hill on the other side of Wolf's property happened to be up late Saturday night when she heard a car driving around the Lambert property. I guess it's quiet out there at night. So she turned her telescope—"

"Her *telescope?*"

"That's right. She's got a telescope trained on the place— I'd bet anything she bought that when she heard what kind of films Wolf was making down there. Anyway, she reports seeing a very large woman poking around the rows of barrels where you found the body. She's tentatively identified Thelma."

"What about this Carlo Baron? Maybe he had some reason to want his son-in-law dead, and he is only next door."

"That's exactly what we need an investigation to find out. This is an area that is traditionally very conservative. A lot of the older residents are Italian or Swiss, if you can believe it. Some Armenian or Portuguese. Religious, mostly Catholic, mostly white. They weren't crazy about having Wolf Lambert making the kind of movies he makes. Now that it's become known that Thelma is branching out and making those films in the neighborhood near where their kids go to school—well, that wasn't exactly the answer to the prayers of the local parents."

"So that was general knowledge?"

"Baronsville is a small town. They've only got a weekly newspaper, but they put out a special edition on the murder. The nearest big paper, the *Santa Rosa Press Democrat*, covered Thelma's trip to the police department in today's issue, and she was identified not only as an actress in the videos, but also as a producer and director. I'm expecting the national media to be around soon. Thelma's been getting death threats already. I'm expecting a groundswell of criticism against her. Baronsville does not welcome this kind of attention—being known as a town where adult videos are filmed."

"I can't imagine any town in America would welcome that."

She spread her hands out, "Let's just say that some places, like the one we're sitting in, take a more live-and-let-live attitude."

"Except for the slight problem that hardly anyone can actually afford to live here."

"Yes, but if they can afford the rent, the expression is free."

We both laughed. She held up a hand, "In the interests of full disclosure, I have to say that our senior partner Bud Harkness has a winery not far from the Lambert spread, but he's one of the liberal San Francisco refugees. We're tolerated there and our money is happily accepted."

I stared at her for a moment. "How did you get involved?"

"Bud Harkness called me in—yesterday afternoon after Thelma called him. Of course, as an associate, I was working on Sunday, anyway. He asked me to get over to the Baronsville PD and represent Thelma. So I met her yesterday afternoon for the first time, while the Baronsville police were questioning her. For what it's worth, I like her."

"I like her, too. I'm just curious, is anyone trying to contact the Manx brothers about all this?"

"The what?"

"Have you talked to the Manx brothers—Rod and Ringo? They were there the day she was arrested, and they were there with her at Wolf Lambert's winery when I discovered the body." It suddenly seemed to me that I was yelling. I gulped and looked around to see if anyone had heard me, but the place was still deserted. The waitress had gone back into the kitchen. "Didn't Thelma mention the Manx brothers? It seemed to me really odd that they took off the moment the police arrived."

Sedona had taken out a yellow legal pad and begun making notes. "I spoke to Thelma this morning, but next time I call, I'll ask her about the—what is it, Marx brothers?"

"Manx brothers. That's what she called them when Thelma introduced me to them. Rod and Ringo. She said she had stolen them away from Wolf." I described the scene at the winery and the next day at the house when Thelma had been arrested.

"You see, Josephine, I didn't know any of this."

"Call me Jo."

"Okay, Jo, if you call me Sedona."

"That's an unusual name."

She smiled, "That's a tactful way to ask. When I was doing poverty law in Alabama, people would get in my face and say, 'What *are* you, anyway?' My father was Sansei, you know, third-generation Japanese American. He was a navy pilot and my mother was from Hawaii—what she called hapa haole. You know what that is? She was born in Hawaii, half Japanese and half Caucasian. My father was stationed there, and that's where my parents met. My mother was very New Age—you know, crystals, incense, tapes of the rain forest. Her favorite place in the world was Sedona, Arizona. My father really had a choice of those two names. My father always said he was tempted to name me after the battleship *Arizona*. I learned how to assert myself very early in life."

"Have you ever been to Sedona, Arizona?"

"So far I've managed to avoid it. I was born and raised here in the Bay Area—my parents wanted to get away from their in-laws—but not too far. And my mother was almost as comfortable here as she could be outside of Sedona." Her smile faltered a little. "She died several months ago, and I promised her I'd scatter her ashes there, so I guess I have to go—after all these years of resisting it."

"I'm sorry for your loss. I was thirteen when my mother died. You don't ever actually get over it, but it does get easier with time."

"I think I am getting better." She drank some of her tea. "Back to Thelma. She has been telling me a lot of things about Wolf Lambert's operation. But so far everything she's said just goes to show that Lambert is erratic and disorganized. As a lawyer I couldn't help thinking maybe she should have gotten some kind of palimony arrangement considering that she was sleeping with him as well as working with him. But she doesn't seem to bear a grudge, and as far as the man whose body was found in the barrel, Thelma scarcely knew him."

"Wolf might have enemies, and this Steve guy might be one of them." I told her about the bizarre amends form-letter I had gotten. "I wonder if the murder victim got one of those."

"You see, Jo, this is why we need your help to get an investigator. There is no way that Thelma can pay for it. Harkness is doing her a big favor by giving me the case. I'm an associate and I don't cost as much as some of the big guns, but nonetheless, donating my time shows you how highly Bud thinks of Thelma. The best thing would be to clear her before they get to the point of making an arrest."

"So your firm wouldn't incur too much expense."

"It's one thing for them to donate my time to Thelma's case. They'd be paying me, anyway. But coughing up cash to pay a private investigator a couple of hundred a day, plus travel—Bud Harkness wants to help Thelma with representation, but not to spend actual money."

"I like Thelma, and I will ask Mrs. Madrone's assistant if there is any way we can help. But frankly, I'm not too optimistic. She's my boss and usually she tells me what to do with my time rather than vice versa. I'll let you know what she says."

"Thank you." The sandwiches came and we started to eat, but I had a sudden thought, "You know San Francisco so well, but I noticed from your bio on the firm web site that you had been working in Alabama until recently."

She nodded with a mouthful of meatloaf sandwich, either in confirmation or approval of my research. "That's true. But I was born here in the city and I've always come back here whenever I could. That's why I accepted the offer from Bud

Harkness to join their firm. I did some work in Alabama that came to their attention. I got an unexpectedly large settlement in a contingency case. Talk about your unethical nonprofits— they not only bilked people who donated money, they tried to get the people who worked for them to join their religious sect. They won't make that mistake again. I wasn't very popular in Alabama, though, after I won that case. When Harkness thought I could be an addition to their firm I jumped at the chance. But that's not what you were asking."

"Not exactly. I just wondered how you knew about that storefront where you picked me up earlier—Friend in Need."

"It's none of my business, but I hope you weren't visiting that place for personal reasons."

"Just getting information."

"I think they're very damaging. They have offices in low-income areas and over in the Sunset district near a couple of colleges. They advertise big time in student newspapers as if they were offering real pregnancy counseling."

"But, as I just discovered, they're actually antiabortion counselors."

"That's right. They say they also offer postabortion counseling, but it boils down to preaching at them to avoid sex. They won't even offer information on contraception, let alone direct women to where they can get real help. They just want to victimize women when they're at their most vulnerable and push their own agenda."

I sighed. "Damn. It sounds like I'm in for a fun week investigating them. I'm just getting as much information as I can at this point."

"Okay. One thing I can tell you is that the storefront there is becoming notorious as a place where antiabortionists mass to go picket legitimate women's health care clinics and harass women going in, on the theory that they just might be getting abortions. I've spent many a Sunday as a volunteer escort taking women through a gauntlet of hate they put up."

"Even here in San Francisco?"

"Oh, I'm sure they regard our fair liberal city as a challenge."

"So they may already have your license plate from some previous encounter."

"It's a possibility. Defending people who are powerless from brainwashing and manipulation by predators is part of the reason I became a lawyer." She put down her sandwich and stared at me. "My God, I hope the Madrone Foundation isn't giving them any money!"

"I can't say. It isn't my decision or my money. But thanks for giving me an idea what to look for; the next place on my list is over on Irving."

"See what I mean? Look at the map and you'll see that's an easy bus ride from City College, UCSF, and SF State." She looked at me intently, as if she wanted to ask something, but instead she looked at her watch. "Would you mind if I dropped you on the K streetcar line? It will take you right down to Irving and I need to drive up to Baronsville to talk to Thelma."

We exchanged business cards. She insisted on paying and I let her. She dropped me off on Market Street with instructions to go down the BART-Muni stairway. I promised to call her after I'd had a chance to talk to my superiors. As I was getting out of the car she leaned over and tapped my arm, "I had considered not telling you this—the police aren't releasing it yet, but Bud Harkness knows some people at the DA's office there. They think they found the murder weapon along with twenty pounds of white powder in a plastic bag concealed in one of the portable lavatories on Wolf Lambert's property."

"What kind of white powder?"

"The initial tests indicate cocaine."

"What's the murder weapon? I thought I saw ligature marks on his neck."

Sedona froze, leaning across the seat for a second. "You're a cold one. Finding a dead body and noticing something like that."

I didn't know what to say. A car behind her honked. Sedona retreated back behind the wheel. Now I had to lean in the door a little to hear her. "Some kind of blunt force trauma to the head, and just outside the lavatory they found a rock that looks like it might have forensic evidence—those tests will take a while."

"This lavatory, was it up on top of a grassy hill in an area that has a gazebo?"

"It might have been. I'll check. Why do you ask?"

I thought of the two men in the Jaguar coming down from the hilltop. "I'll tell you later."

She nodded thoughtfully.

I wondered if Wolf was involved somehow, either directly or as a target.

I rode the N-Judah light-rail car over to Irving and got off in the middle of a bustling neighborhood with apartment buildings squeezed in next to health food stores, video rental stores, trendy restaurants, and produce markets. The traffic was intense. A parked car began to pull out of a space and another car squealed to a stop and double-parked, waiting to pull into the spot. Other drivers stacked up behind. One driver honked and pulled around to pass, nearly flattening an elderly couple in a crosswalk at the intersection.

The Friend in Need office was above a martial arts studio. This version was more expensively furnished. It had a doctor's office look about it, with a low table stacked with magazines in front of an upholstered sofa and chairs. Rather than a counter with a frosted window, there was a small wooden desk guarding a door to an inner office. Sitting behind the wooden desk was the woman with the platinum blond hair and the bubble gum pink sweater. This time she had dropped that expression of sincere concern.

"I expected to see you. That's why I came over here. What are you doing, harassing us?" she asked. I noticed that she had a huge diamond ring on her finger and a sweet Southern accent that clashed with the harsh words.

"Well, now it sounds like you folks are no strangers to the art of harassment," I said, irritable that it had gotten so confrontational so quickly.

The blonde stood up and came around the counter. "I saw you with that Oriental woman. We know who she is. She is out to spoil our work—and you. You're not even with child, are you? Of course not. You couldn't be. No man would have you."

I stared at her in astonishment. She was several inches shorter than my five foot eight—probably about five two, and very petite. An unpleasant smile spread over her features. "I can't blame you. You just don't know God's will. It's never too late. I have a special message for you. I haven't brought it here because that woman—" she spat out the words. "She destroyed my mission back in Alabama. But I still help people when I can." She went back behind the desk and reached into what looked like a very expensive leather handbag and pulled out a bright pink flyer. "Take this. Go home, read it and call me if you want to talk. I think you should go now. I'll pray for you." It was a dismissal.

Speechless, I turned to go. Then, I had a sudden thought and reached into my purse. The woman's face collapsed into terror. She probably thought I was going for a gun, but I took out the small camera Harvey and Wally had given me and focused on the blonde.

"Smile." I took a couple of flash pictures of her. Then I turned on my heel and walked out. I dropped the camera in my purse along with the pink flyer. There was no sense in taking any of the Friend in Need flyers—I already had them from the previous visit.

I made my way back to Pine Street and dressed up a little for dinner.

A Ton of Trouble

The restaurant was only a few blocks away, but climbing the lower slopes of Nob Hill made it seem more of an expedition than it looked like on the map. Ambrose arrived at the door at the same moment, but he hadn't broken a sweat. I would have asked what his exercise regimen was, but I was afraid he would tell me.

Ambrose recommended the prix fixe, four-course dinner. Over the excellent cream-of-celery soup and the salad, I told him about the wine expert in the BMW and he smiled sadly. "He was probably so busy telling everyone else what to think the wine was wasted on him. Does Lambert's Lair have good wine?"

"You know, I didn't try any of it."

"Typical, Jo. If you go to a winery, you should at least taste the wines."

"Next time, I will. Look, I'm tasting this one."

"Well, it's a start."

I told him what Sedona Yamada had told me about the Friend in Need offices—and about Thelma's situation.

There was a pause while he took in the information. "Thank god, Mrs. Madrone is on her way to Paris, so you'll have some time to sort all this out. I hope I didn't just hear you say that you disapprove of the grant candidate she wants you to investigate—an organization dedicated to promoting motherhood. And that you are going to suggest your own candidate—protecting a pornographic film star. What is wrong with this picture?"

We both laughed. "When you put it that way, it doesn't sound very promising."

"I would strongly advise you not to put it any way at all. Jo, I have observed Mrs. Madrone enough over the years to know that she would never finance you to investigate for that poor, unfortunate porn actress."

"You're pretty sure she wouldn't be interested."

"I'll go as far as to say I don't think it would be a good idea to even mention it. As far as the Friend in Need offices, just go there, get the information, and explain why you recommend whatever it is you do recommend."

"Okay, thanks." The entrees arrived, Muscovy duck in rosemary sauce for Ambrose, while I had broiled sea bass. We ate in silence. The food was so good that this wasn't much of a hardship, but I couldn't resist saying, "Um, Ambrose, I confess, I expected a more liberal response."

"It's my job to protect Mrs. Madrone. My own opinions don't have to be identical to hers. I will say that at least we don't have to worry about exploiting the opposite sex in the gay community. Anatomy is destiny in gay porn. You know I'm talking about consenting adults, of course?" But he made it a question.

"Yes."

"Good because you'd be surprised how many otherwise intelligent, but totally uninformed, people seem to think gay porn means molesting children."

"Do people really believe that?"

"Some people prefer prejudice to facts."

"Oh, yeah. I've met some of those people."

Ambrose took another sip of wine and regarded me solemnly. "I've known sex workers."

My face must have shown surprise, "You . . ."

"Don't look at me like that—not in the exercise of their profession. If you must know, I met a man who was in a couple of classes I took. I was surprised to see him later on the box of an adult video I was considering renting."

A Ton of Trouble

"What kind of classes if I may be so bold as to ask?"

"Two kinds of classes actually," Ambrose smiled mischievously, well aware that his private life was something of a mystery to me. "I'm a serious student of fencing. I also take ballet classes, and the occasional tai chi class. This boy was in both fencing and ballet—which is quite unusual, so I had reason to recognize his photograph immediately. He was also quite attractive, which didn't hurt. I asked him about it later, and it turned out he not only did the films, but also made money on the gay strip circuit."

I drank a little wine and contemplated this new information. "I guess Thelma couldn't do that. Large-sized porn is such a fringe market, there isn't any strip circuit."

Ambrose patted my arm, "You never know, dear. If there are enough people to buy videos, maybe there's a whole audience of closet cases who just haven't come out yet."

"You're just saying that to cheer me up. Besides, I have very little in common with most of the people I've met who are involved with the plus-sized porn—except being in favor of size acceptance."

"Welcome to the world of gay bars."

I finished my wine and surveyed the remains of the excellent dinner. "So what happened with this sex worker guy? Did you, um . . . ?"

"We never got involved, if that's what you're asking. But we did become friends for a while. He has a rather short attention span and I'm always traveling, so we've never gotten terribly close. I still see him from time to time in one class or another."

Along with the sublime food, I was absorbing all this new information about Ambrose, so I just nodded. "I appreciate your advice about Mrs. Madrone. I guess I won't mention it to her."

"I have my own vested interest in keeping you working here. If you left, I'd just have to break in a new investigator."

"Hmm, well, aside from the exquisite crème brûlée, I notice that they have key lime pie on the menu, so I'll be back here again before I leave town."

"Let me know, I love an excuse to come to this place."

"What about your friend who didn't get to go to that cottage? If he's back in town soon, you could bring him."

"Perhaps." This time when Ambrose smiled there was a definite Mona Lisa quality to it.

It wasn't late when I walked back to the Pine Street condo. Back in the room, I called Sedona Yamada and explained that sources close to Mrs. Madrone had made it clear that funding an investigation for Thelma was not possible. I didn't mention Ambrose's name. I wasn't sure just how much Sedona knew about his position, and Ambrose always preferred giving out less information where Mrs. Madrone was concerned.

"Look, I'm not asking you to commit yourself," Sedona said. "But could you come up to Baronsville and talk to Thelma? I'll give you her phone number. It would mean a lot."

"Maybe I could fit it in tomorrow."

I was too restless to settle down, so I looked at the materials I had gathered from my day of visiting the Friend in Need offices. The rose-petal-and-bunny-bedecked flyers with the gory pictures inside were pretty much what I had expected.

The blonde had given me a similar flyer that appeared to offer services for unwed mothers-to-be, on paper tinted a brighter pink, with her business card attached. It appeared that her name was Raylene Shotwell and she and her husband operated a thriving church as well as some church-sponsored counseling services. The contact information was all in Alabama. None of it explained what she was doing in California. I put it next to my laptop computer to investigate later. As an afterthought I took out the small camera and put it on top of the literature.

I realized that Mulligan hadn't called me when he got back to Seattle. I could have called to see how the cats were doing. I could have called the building manager, Maxine, listened to her macaw shriek in the background, and gotten confirmation that Mulligan had arrived safely. But that would have given Maxine the information that Mulligan hadn't called me himself. In the end I called no one, and spent some time staring out the condo's window at some rooftops and a small patch of San Francisco Bay.

Thelma's tiny apartment in Baronsville was immaculately tidy. There was a small home office area with computer, file cabinet, and an excellent large-sized ergonomic office chair. Thelma greeted me at the door and led the way to a pair of easy chairs that flanked a sofa.

She seemed subdued. "Hi, shall I call you Thelma? Or would you prefer to be called Mandy?"

"I don't know what I want. Everyone I've met in recent years calls me Thelma, including accounting clients, if I still have any. So you might as well call me that."

The phone rang. Thelma just looked at it. On the second ring her message machine asked anyone who wanted a return call or who needed bookkeeping services to leave a message. I flinched to hear the venom in the voice that came on the line, "You fat slut. You should be ashamed. We don't need your kind here. This was a decent community before you came. You make me sick. Go to hell where you belong. By the way, I know where you live and I have a shotgun. Watch your back."

"That's a keeper," Thelma said, removing the message tape, inserting a fresh one, and dropping the one from the machine into a large envelope entitled "Death Threats." She noted the date and time on the tape label. I peeked into the envelope and saw that there were five or six other tapes in it.

"You're so methodical."

She smiled, "I can't help it. I'm that way about everything. And I do mean everything." She rolled her eyes and giggled a little, and I realized she was referring to her film career. The woman was incorrigible.

"Those are all death threats?"

"Mostly. Some are just obscene and say they're going to come over and do something hurtful but not necessarily fatal. The police told me they'd check them out. I don't know if that's true, but I'm making copies for my lawyer as well, just in case. Hell, it's not like my accounting business is booming right now."

"Have you lost a lot of clients?"

She sighed, "Many of my long-term clients have been very loyal. But I haven't had any new business since this story broke. I don't know what I'm going to do if this keeps up."

She settled into one of the chairs. "Would you like some coffee or tea?" A thermal carafe sat on the coffee table with cups, instant coffee, creamer, and tea bags. I accepted a cup of peppermint tea and some sugar to put in it. I was unexpectedly touched that Thelma had set this up in advance of my visit.

"How are you holding up—last time I saw you, you were on your way to talk to the police. How did that go?"

"Sedona called it a fishing expedition. I think they wanted to intimidate me. But I'm not guilty of anything. I don't think they believed me."

"Did you actually know this Steve? The guy in the barrel."

"Steve Farquar. I met him when he came to Wolf's. He never wasted more than a few minutes talking to me. Wolf wouldn't usually bother to see him."

"Did he have some kind of business with Wolf?"

"Carlo Baron was trying to buy the vineyards back. He lives next door and the whole thing used to be a family property, but his father had a gambling problem and sold a lot of it. Carlo has been buying it back and he wants Wolf's place, but it's not for sale. A man like Baron doesn't take no for an answer, but he also doesn't want to keep hearing it. So he sent Steve around to bother Wolf about it very few days."

"And you say Wolf wouldn't see him?"

"He talked to him once or twice, but finally, he just told me to tell Steve he wasn't interested."

"But Steve kept coming around?"

"He didn't have much choice if he wanted to keep working for his father-in-law. He would joke about it every time he stopped and I told him Wolf wasn't available. Sometimes he'd stay a few minutes and flirt with Heather. But if I stayed in the room and watched, he'd get nervous and leave." She smiled wickedly.

"Did you see him that day, the day we found his body?"

The smile vanished. "No. I haven't seen him since I stopped working for Wolf several weeks back. Heather might have let Steve hang around a little more, silly girl."

"What about Wolf? Have you seen him recently?"

"No, but we talk most days. In fact I spoke to him a few minutes ago. He's home from the hospital and very anxious to talk to you."

"To me?"

"The police suspect him as much as they suspect me. Sedona said she told you about the cocaine they found on his property. Something tells me the police aren't going to look very hard if they can get rid of two pornographers—frame me for murder, and frame Wolf for drugs."

"You say 'frame' Wolf for drugs, but he does have a substance abuse problem. Are you sure that the cocaine they found wasn't his?"

"You never can be one hundred percent sure about anyone. But even when he was drinking, I never saw Wolf use cocaine, and goodness knows he doesn't have a very secretive disposition." Thelma spread her hands in helplessness. "I slept with him, I lived with him, and I never noticed him hiding anything. That's all I can say."

"Okay." I nodded.

Thelma leaned forward. "Sedona tried to get your employer to fund an investigation. I'll bet Mrs. Madrone said no."

"In essence she did. She is a very conservative older woman. Her charitable projects are personal to her."

"I could have told Sedona that. But Wolf has an idea. He asked me if you'd consider stopping by the winery before you leave Baronsville today."

"Maybe I can do that." I hesitated. "Can I ask an impertinent question?"

"Join the crowd."

"Why did you get into this adult-film thing?"

Thelma laughed. "What's a nice fat girl like you doing . . . ? Never mind. I could see the police wanted to ask that too, but they didn't. I confess—Wolf Lambert was not my first explicit-video experience."

"Really?"

"If you could see your face!" Thelma laughed uproariously. "Sorry," she said, wiping her eyes. "I was going out with a man who showed me his collection of porn featuring big women. He told me I was prettier than any of those women. I said, why not? So we made an audition tape. I am shocking you, aren't I?"

"Let's just say, I wouldn't do it. I'm not judging you for doing it, but I do suspect the motives of that boyfriend."

Thelma sighed, "I'm sure my ex-boyfriend had some idea of becoming a porn star himself, or at the very least being my manager and making some money. He didn't last past the audition tape. There are three things a man needs to have to be a porn star."

She waited.

"Okay, go ahead and tell me. What are they?"

"First, he has to have impressive equipment—it has to show up on film, right? Second, he has to be able to maintain an erection throughout any distraction—strangers, lights, stopping and starting. Third, he has to climax on demand. Can you guess where my ex-boyfriend fell short?"

I shook my head.

"All of the above." Thelma collapsed into giggles, and I found myself laughing as well. "I agree with you. He was using me. But it was mutual. The audition tape led to a part in a film that Wolf saw. Then Wolfie offered me a job. His films were better, and when I started doing his books I even got medical and dental insurance."

"You're a bookkeeper. Couldn't you make more money at that if you applied yourself?"

Thelma looked at me in silence for a moment. "Have you ever had the experience of interviewing over the telephone for a job and having them tell you that you are exactly what they want—the job is yours—and then when you go in to meet them, wearing your conservative interview suit and, God help you, queen-sized pantyhose and heels, they take one look at you and say, 'I'm sorry but since we talked the position has been filled.' Have you ever had that experience?"

"That happened to you?"

"That happened to me more than once."

"Is that legal?"

"Ask a lawyer. I did. He said I didn't have grounds to sue because it's perfectly legal to discriminate against me. Even if they told me in front of witnesses, or put it on paper that they weren't hiring me because I'm fat, I would have no grounds to sue them."

"I didn't know that."

"I'm not even going to get into all the social rejection I've suffered, Jo. You're big enough yourself that you might have gone through some of that as well. But on the other side of it, there are men like Wolf who want me because of my size. That was an eye-opener. I don't know why it should take a man's desire to make me feel good about myself, but it did." She riveted me with an intense blue-eyed stare. "Sex made me feel human."

I gulped at the force behind the words. "Um, okay."

Thelma laughed. "So, maybe I do have a very strong sex drive, and a bit of an exhibitionist streak. When I did that first video, I liked the idea of flaunting it in people's faces. Having men and even some women want me made me feel powerful. I was looking for a way out of that relationship, and the thought even crossed my mind that making an X-rated movie might be a good way to meet men who might appreciate my, uh, natural endowments. It happened, too. Wolf gave me lots of opportunities." She sighed. "But . . ."

"But . . ."

"When I meet men they want to meet the goddess, Thelma T—the Ton of Trouble, they don't want to meet Mandy Hanson from Modesto."

"A good man is hard to find."

"Tell me about it. You seem to have found one."

"I'm working on it." I let it go at that.

"Well, I hope you make a go of it. If you get tired of him, send him round here—if I'm not in prison by then."

Both of us were silent for a moment.

"You haven't seen my films yet, have you?"

"Uh, no."

"I'd like to give you a copy, but I'm embarrassed to say I don't have any! All the newspaper coverage has driven up the demand. But if you'd like I can call Maurice and have him save you a copy. He's just outside of Baronsville on Highway 12, it's on your way back if you take 12 toward 101 after you visit Wolf, you can't miss it, it's the Blue Movie Store, he sells adult books and videos. It's a great store. Very cozy, you won't feel threatened, I mean the floors aren't sticky and there aren't a bunch of booths with men doing suspicious things behind the curtains."

"Maybe another time."

"But you will see Wolf today?"

"All right."

"Can I call Wolf and tell him you're coming?"

In the end, I couldn't turn down a visit to Wolf Lambert. Thelma tried to call him for several minutes before she got through. "Reporters camping on his line," she muttered. After she finally got Wolf on the phone she told him I would be right over.

"Tell him I can't stay long."

"That's fine. Go. I told him you were on your way."

A crowd of cars clustered around the winery gate, which was shut and locked. Several cars displayed press parking permits, and there was a van from a local television station with strange hardware on top. I realized that this was pretty big news.

I drove slowly through the crowd of reporters on foot. One of them reached out to grab at my windshield, and for a horrific moment I thought he was going to break off a windshield wiper, but he backed away.

Someone called out, "Josephine Fuller!" and I stared out my side window for a moment. I wouldn't have said that any reporter knew my name, but one of them did. Now everyone did. Great.

I didn't have any strategies for getting in, but the very tall, hatchet-faced man I had seen outside the warehouse waved me up to the gate and carefully opened it for me to drive through, then clanged it shut in the faces of the reporters, who drifted back to their original posts like disappointed piranha sniffing the waters for fresh blood elsewhere.

Seen up close, the man who had let me through the gate was impressively tall, definitely taller than Ambrose. He must have been six foot six at least. He paced along easily beside my slow-moving car. When I parked and got out, he came over and stood in front of me.

"My name is Arthur Terhune, I'm the wine maker here." The way he said it made me realize that it was a title. He held out a hand as if it pained him to make my acquaintance.

I introduced myself.

"Yes," he said mournfully. "We're expecting you, would you come through here." I followed him through the tasting room, the office, and through a side door I hadn't seen before into the residence part of the house. Terhune looked back at me. "I'm hoping you won't tire him out too much. He almost died, and it wasn't his fault."

"You mean he didn't purposely mix Antabuse and alcohol?"

"He took an herbal cold remedy with alcohol in it. It was a mistake, but it could have killed him. Having those jackals outside the gate hasn't helped at all. You can see why you should make it a brief visit."

"Believe me, that was my plan all along."

Terhune opened the door and stood aside to let me go through.

Wolf Lambert was sitting on a sofa with his feet up and an assortment of blankets and afghan throws draped over him in layers. He looked pale and wearied, his smile was a shadow of his usual buoyant spirits. He gestured me in and said hoarsely, "Thank you for coming to see me, sweetheart, I'm feeling a little under the weather."

I went to shake his hand and he captured my hand and kissed it. "Sit down, doll. I won't keep you long, I have a favor to ask."

"I'm glad you're feeling better. I was worried about you." I sat, prudently out of arm's reach, in a suede upholstered rocking chair near the sofa.

"I apologize for our last meeting, doll. I have no recollection of it whatsoever, but I understand it was right up there with my top ten blackouts of the decade. And to think I didn't even have the dubious pleasure of driving myself down there with fine wine." He shook his head.

"If you hadn't knocked that barrel out of the way, it might have taken a few days longer to find that man's body."

"Yes, that's true. The man was a nuisance, but his death is a colossal disaster."

The door opened, and a tall, thin woman came in. I guessed her to be in her mid-thirties. One or two gray hairs made it clear her pale blond hair was untouched by dye, but she had a bone-weary way of moving that made her seem much older. "I brought your tea," she said in a hoarse whisper as if she had been crying or screaming or being strangled.

"Jo, this is Sylvia Terhune, who helps me out around here."

Sylvia flinched as if he had shouted at her. She resembled her father so much that Wolf almost didn't have to introduce me to his housekeeper. Her long, thin face was swollen, as if she had been crying. Considering the hoarse voice, I wondered if she had been wailing as well.

"Hello," I said.

Sylvia put the tray down in front of Wolf. She glanced at

me briefly, then lowered her eyes immediately, "I brought an extra cup. Dad said you had company."

"Thank you, dear." Wolf said gently.

She stood for a second and I noticed the blood seeping through her white sleeve.

"You have blood on your sleeve," I said without thinking. She stared at me.

"Arthur," Wolf said in a fairly loud voice. This time Sylvia didn't flinch. She cringed away from me as if my words had struck her.

"I didn't mean to," she said in that hoarse whisper. Arthur came through the door so quickly that he must have been listening outside. "I felt so bad. I thought it was good for him. It was just herbal cold medicine."

Wolf spoke very quietly to Arthur, but I could hear the word. "Blood."

Sylvia looked up at her father. Arthur came up to her, looked at her sleeve, and put his arm around her shoulder. "Honey, we have to go talk to Dr. Patchen."

"What about Wolf's lunch?"

"Jo will help me. Won't you, Jo?" Wolf appealed to me.

"Sure." I sighed soundlessly. What was I letting myself in for?

Sylvia leaned against her father as if her power to stand had suddenly drained away. Arthur led her from the room.

After the door shut behind them, I asked Wolf, "What did she mean about the herbal cold medicine?"

"She gave me a dose of some kind of tincture of herbs. It wasn't much, but it had alcohol in it and that mixed with the Antabuse . . . Well, I guess you saw the results. I never thought to ask her if there was alcohol in the medicine, because of all that crap about it being homeopathic. It's my fault as much as hers. I should have checked the label, but she blames herself."

"So she cut herself."

Wolf sighed. "It's not the first time. She's getting therapy for it. But, having that little creep killed here on the property didn't help, either. Steve was her first boyfriend—her only boyfriend, I guess. He used to work in the Marketing Department at the Baron Winery. Art was their wine maker, and that's where Steve met Sylvia. When he dropped her for Carlo Baron's daughter, Sylvia reacted by cutting her wrists. She nearly bled to death. That was about the time I convinced her father to work for me. Arthur just couldn't stay at the Baron's, where Sylvia would be tortured by watching Steve lording it up with the boss's daughter.

"Arthur is an artist among wine makers. I offered him and

his daughter a safe refuge, and he was glad to come over here. It really toasted Carlo Baron's chestnuts. Arrogant bastard."

"I thought Steve worked in real estate."

"Baron had to put him somewhere. They tried to put him in the marketing department of their winery, but he had no nose for wine and he tried to steal accounts from the older salesmen. They finally threatened to quit if Carlo didn't remove him. By then he'd married the boss's daughter, so they tried him over in the winery itself and he pissed off the winery workers. They're men who are very conscious of their dignity. If he'd stayed there it would have been only a matter of time before one of those guys nailed him with a pruning knife. He caused less trouble in the real estate office, where he could only terrorize the secretaries."

"No one seems to know how he was killed, or why he was stashed there. But the police must be looking at you carefully. After all, the body was discovered here."

"They can look all they want. I didn't kill him and neither did any of my employees. Why should we?"

I didn't say anything about the cocaine in the Port-a-Pottie. If Thelma knew, he must know about it. But he didn't mention it, either. Perhaps he didn't know. I put it aside for the moment.

"If Sylvia is so fragile, her father must have hated having Steve coming over all the time. Thelma said he used to show up regularly trying to persuade you to sell the property."

Wolf shook his head. "We made sure that Sylvia never saw Steve. She stays pretty close to the living quarters. She's so shy she doesn't want to run into any of the wine-tasting customers. I understand Steve talked to Heather—the receptionist. He was trying to get to me through her." Wolf leaned back in his chair. "Steve was a pain in the ass but ineffectual. Thelma used to just tell him to shove off. He was afraid of Thelma. I really miss her."

He finished his tea. I looked at him a little uncertainly. Not sure how much of an invalid he was.

"Can I get you something? Sylvia said you needed lunch."

"Would you mind taking the tray back into the kitchen, dear? I'll show you where it is. I'd carry it myself, but I'm just a little shaky today and I don't want to drop it. That would upset Sylvia even more." He got up and led the way into the kitchen. He did seem unsteady on his feet, and he held on to the door frame when we went into the kitchen. It was a lovely peaceful room, with a long wooden table and a sliding glass door that let in light and opened onto a patio with a grape arbor overhead and a table and chairs.

"Just put the cups in the sink. If I can get you to make us a sandwich, perhaps you might join me."

I asked him what he wanted and found bread and cheese, tomatoes and mayonnaise and made us some sandwiches. I winced a little wielding the kitchen knives as I thought of Sylvia wielding them on herself. I made it a point to wash them and put them back in their holders immediately. Wolf asked for apple juice with his sandwich and I had some, too.

Sitting at the table with Lambert had an unexpectedly domestic feeling about it.

"You know, the wine business might not be the best thing for someone with a drinking problem," I said, throwing tact to the wind.

Wolf blinked at me in surprise. I hadn't meant to hurt or anger him. He shook his head sadly and said, "I've lived here for fifteen years now, I'm not about to leave."

"Okay. So you wouldn't sell to Carlo Baron. You said his grandfather was a bootlegger. Are you in any danger that he might, um, make you an offer you can't refuse."

Wolf chuckled. "Maybe I shouldn't have asked to see you, babe, you may be too much for my system all at once. When Carlo first started bothering me, I checked with some of my connections and he's fairly legit. He's not going to send some clown to break my kneecaps if I don't sell. The serious mobsters think of this as a very admirable little crusade he's got, buying back the family land, but it's not business. Those guys only use violence in the name of money. I'm not saying that Carlo wouldn't scare me into selling if he thought he could do it and still keep his nose clean. When he first started sending the kid around, that might have been his plan. But the little squirt was just annoying. I think Carlo was sending him here as much to punish him as anything."

"Why would he want to punish him?"

"Why would anyone want to punish their son-in-law? I'm hoping you can dig around, go to their realty office in Baronsville, see what you can find. You can even ask Heather. She was the one who listened to him. They must have talked about something. Everyone else here was happy to ignore him."

"Someone didn't ignore him."

"That's right, and I want to pay for your time and expenses to find out why."

"Isn't that a job better suited to the local police?"

"With all due respect to the Baronsville Police Department, they're a small local unit with limited resources. There are some areas where I am sure the police won't be looking. They can tie the body to this property so, of course, they are examining my affairs with a microscope."

"Not to mention a telescope. Did you know your neighbor up on the hill reported seeing Thelma poking around those barrels the night Steve was killed?"

"I know the neighbor you're talking about. It wouldn't hurt if you can get a look at that back deck with the telescope. Let me see if I can arrange for you to get up there."

"Wolf, I don't think I can promise—"

"You know the Baronsville police won't be able to track down the Manx brothers in the wilds of LA, for example."

"I hope you don't think I'm able to do something like that."

He held up his hand. "And I will suggest that the local police talk to them. But they have no reason to believe the Manx brothers are even involved, and they're not going to go chasing all over to find Rod and Ringo, just on the off chance that they might know something useful."

"Do you have a reason to think they might be involved?"

"I'm not sure, but you told Thelma you saw them running away just about the time the police arrived to talk to her. She really needs your help and so do I, dear." He reached out and grabbed my hand. Damn, I had thought I was out of reach, but he was more agile than his pale appearance suggested.

"All right." I pulled free of his grip. "If I help you, it will have to be in my spare time, because I am here in the Bay Area to do a job for Mrs. Madrone."

"By all means, honey. Perhaps you can just check that realty office in Baronsville on your way back home. Let me know as soon as you can spare a day, and you can go down and see the Manx brothers in LA?"

"You know where they are?"

"The San Fernando Valley is the capital of porn, darling. I can give you a couple of people to call when you get there, and they'll find the Manx brothers. They've got to live, and those boys do that by screwing anything that moves."

"So, they don't, um, specialize, the way you do?"

"No, that's why I stopped using them. They were disrespectful to my actresses. I won't have that. I warned Thelma that there was a great deal of hostility mixed in with their performances. But they are ambitious—not everyone has the kind of skills to do that kind of work."

"Please don't tell me. I think Thelma told me enough."

"Let's just say they have to perform on cue in every sense of the word, in the face of every kind of distraction, and those boys were reliable. Thelma was offering them both money and a chance to get some directorial credit."

"But you don't know of any connection between them and this Steve, the murdered man?"

"That's why I want you to talk to them and find out."

"If they are murderers, they're hardly likely to tell me, and it might be dangerous to talk to them."

"I'll pay for some backup. Hire anyone you want and send me the bill. You don't have to go alone. It's just that I trust you. Believe me, I know you can hire people, but finding people with brains and integrity is not accomplished simply by throwing money at something. This is my life and my home. Thelma is someone I love. I don't want to lose it all. Please help me."

"I'll do my best, but I am not about to jeopardize a job I care about by shortchanging my boss."

"Of course not."

"Thelma wants me to go to some sort of smut shop and now you're sending me over to the real estate company. I've only got so much time to spare. Okay?"

"Smut shop—that must be Newburn's Blue Movie Store

on the edge of town. I highly recommend it." He gave me directions and I wrote them down.

I had my notebook out to write down the address and I noticed the piece of winery stationery I'd picked up next to the gazebo on top of the hill.

I showed it to Wolf. "Do you know anything about this?"

He looked at it and raised his eyebrows, *"Gloria, Anita, Teri, Jeff, Ivan, 1983–86 Cheryl and Maria???, Lillian, Mandy, Art, Sylvia, Angie—more?"*

He held out his hand and I gave it to him. "This is my amends list. Where did you find it?"

"Up on the hill next to the gazebo."

"That's odd. I've been looking for it in my desk down in the winery. It got separated from the draft of my letter." He smiled sheepishly. "They told me Heather sent that out to most of the people on our mailing list."

"Right. I got one."

"I'm so sorry. Anyway, thanks for bringing this back. My memory isn't what it used to be and I don't want to forget anyone." He folded it and put it in his pocket. I was glad I had made a copy. "This time I'll write the letters myself."

"Do you think any of the people on that list might have had reason to harm you?"

"Maybe. But I don't think any of them knew Steve Farquar."

"Sylvia knew him." I regretted it immediately.

"She's not capable of something like that. She can barely get through the day." Wolf sighed. "Anything else you'd like to discuss?"

"I'm assuming you know what they found in that Port-a-Pottie up near the gazebo."

"The DEA officials mentioned it while they were going

over my property with a fine-tooth comb. They didn't find anything else because there wasn't anything else to find. Someone planted that. But thank you for that much trust, anyway," his voice was ironic, but I noticed that he was looking at the table sadly.

"It sounds to me like someone was trying to cast suspicion on you. It might help to know who the people on the list are."

"You already know that Thelma is Mandy."

"And I met Sylvia and Art."

"Yes. You did meet Sylvia and Art. I'll think about the rest and let you know. Now, when you go to Maurice's, see if you can get my masterpiece, *Big Top Thelma*—it has a sort of Fellini circus kind of effect—only with real hardcore action . . ."

I wasn't thrilled at the prospect. "These films are expensive."

"Tell Maurice to put it on my account. You can go to the real estate place another day."

"I'll go tomorrow. It's too late today." I left muttering, and feeling like a pushover.

The reporters cars were still outside the gate when I left, although the TV van was no longer visible. Now several people were calling my name. Great. They had heard whoever it was call me by name. A very short, auburn-haired sunburned man hammered at the driver's side window as I drove slowly through the gate. He stuffed a business card down under the car's windshield wiper, deep into the well.

I kept waiting for the wind to take it off the car as I drove back to San Francisco, but even crossing the Golden Gate Bridge, I could see its little white edge. When I reached the parking garage under the Pine Street condo, I retrieved the card. It read, "Jerry Buck, Reporter, *National Interrogator*."

A Ton of Trouble

The shock was not that I should get a card from a reporter for the sleazy supermarket tabloid. I was surprised at myself. I actually had met the man before. On the reverse he had written, "I owe you breakfast and I have information for you."

"Sure you do," I said to myself skeptically, but I put the card in my notebook just in case.

W hen I got up the next morning I looked at the list of
places Mrs. Madrone wanted me to investigate. They
were all Friend in Need branch offices—in various suburbs
of San Francisco. I decided to do a facilities check and literature inventory. One was in Petaluma, and I could easily
expand the day to include a stop at the Baronsville real estate
company owed by Carlo Baron. I called Thelma first to ask if
the property they had been using to shoot their video was
managed by the Baronsville firm. It was not. She gave me the
owner's number and I called to explain that I wanted something to dangle in front of the Carlo Baron's staff so that they
would talk to me.

The owner laughed at the wording. "Dangle away, honey.
Even if you signed on the dotted line, it wouldn't be legally
binding because I keep my own staff to manage my property.
If they call, I'll tell them you're authorized to get information
for me. Just let me know if there's anything else I can do to
help. Thelma is a sweet baby, and I don't want her hassled."

The Baronsville real estate office turned out to be almost
deserted. The receptionist didn't look twenty-one, with huge
dark eyes, delicate features, and a mane of dark curls falling
over a face swollen with tears. The brass plaque on her desk

read Fawn Morgan, and the name seemed appropriate. She dipped into a huge box of tissues, had the red-eyed, red-nosed look of someone who has just barely got her emotions under control. I wondered what her relationship was with the murdered man. Perhaps everyone working here was a relative.

"Excuse me, I know you have suffered a tragedy. Is the office open for business today?"

The receptionist sniffled, grabbed another tissue and her chin quivered. "Yes." She started to sob. "Most of the family stayed home. The rest of us are just trying to cope."

"It sounds like you're a very caring group of people."

"Yes, excuse me. I'm sorry."

A voice came from the back of the office. "I can help the lady, Fawn."

I walked to the back office where I found a short, thin woman standing in the doorway to an office that had an outside window on a side street. She had short blond hair just a shade lighter than her tanned skin and wore a white turtleneck sweater with a black pantsuit. There were several cardboard banker's boxes on chairs and she had nearly stripped the office of every sign of occupancy except for a 20- by 24-inch gold-framed portrait of a dark haired beauty in a frothy wedding gown and a man with sandy hair in a gray tuxedo.

"The Farquars in happier times?" I asked.

"You can go home, Fawn," the blonde said.

I turned around to see that the receptionist had followed me like an uncertain puppy, clutching a box of tissues. "If you don't mind, Bonnie. I shouldn't have come—I, I, I've got to go home." She fled and I found myself looking into the more hard-bitten face.

"So are you a reporter?"

"No." I introduced myself.

"I'm Bonnie Prescott, the bookkeeper." She had a firm, brief handshake and cold hands. I don't usually talk to clients, but the family is out of the office today on account of the tragedy. You probably read about it in the papers."

"Yes, I'm so sorry. I just need a little information, and I'll come back for the more detailed stuff another time. Is everyone in the office a family member?"

"Except for Fawn and me. Frankly she's taking it worse than the widow."

"I wonder if that's because she's so young, Fawn, I mean."

"Yes, that must be it." Bonnie looked at me steadfastly. I realized that she was angry, but not at me. "If you're not a reporter, are you just here out of morbid curiosity?"

"No. I'm partly here to get some information for a property owner who was considering using your management services."

"And partly what?"

"I happen to know the woman they are suspecting of having done this, and I think she's innocent. She said she only met the man a few times when she was working as Wolf Lambert's bookkeeper." I hoped there was some solidarity among bookkeepers.

"That wasn't what I heard that woman was doing at Lambert's Lair."

"She made some films with him. But she mainly kept his accounts. So, this was Steve's office?" I couldn't help but stare at the wedding picture.

"Yeah." The red-eyed receptionist came out with a shoulder bag and whispered something inaudible. "I'll call you, hon, when I know more."

"Thanks, Bonnie. You're the only one I can trust." Fawn gave her a quick hug and turned and fled out the door, clutching a tissue.

"She's pretty upset," I said slowly. "Did she have a thing going with the guy?"

She glanced around. The office was deserted. She nodded. "Fawn's okay, she's too naive to know any better. But that Steve. I don't care if he is dead, it's a damn shame that that bastard cheated on little Angie."

"Little Angie? The woman in the picture."

"Yes. That's their wedding picture. I've got to stop calling her that. I've just been here since she was a toddler." She put the picture in a box by itself and firmly closed the office door. Then she led me to the front desk where Fawn had been sitting and took the receptionist's chair. She motioned me to sit down in the chair next to the desk. She opened the drawer and brought out another box of tissues and carefully wiped her eyes.

"Forgive me, this is very hard on all of us. Angela Baron used to bring her daughter in and they were like matching dolls. They were so alike so we called them little Angie and big Angie." She sighed, "They both had that stunning dead black hair, green eyes, olive skin. Angela Baron was just gorgeous, and so proud of that cute little daughter. Who knew that Mrs. Baron would gain so much weight." She clapped her hand over her mouth and stared at me.

"It's all right. Those things happen. I am not offended to talk about it."

"It's not you I'm worried about offending. We just don't mention it around here. It's been many years since big Ang— um, Mrs. Baron even left her house. Even the beautician who does her hair goes to her. Shopping, everything, she has it all brought in. In recent years the only place I know she goes is to the Overeaters Anonymous meetings over at the Baronsville Community Center next to the Lutheran Church. Not that it seems to do much good, but my Sandy goes to that church and she saw her coming out of the meeting, so that's how she knows Mrs. Baron goes there."

"Could I get their address? I'd be very interested in their meetings."

"Sure." She gave me the street address and the intersection. "It's very nice. Friendly people." She examined me carefully. "You know just because it hasn't helped big—uh, Mrs. Baron much doesn't mean that it wouldn't help you."

"You never know," I said. The kind of help I wanted from that meeting place was not something I felt like sharing. "Is it just that group or do they have a lot of other twelve-step programs there at the same location?"

"Oh, that's the main place in town for all those meetings. Several evenings a week they have kind of an open house where people can come and sit and talk. Just to socialize a little with no liquor or, um, other temptations. There aren't a lot of activities in this town and it's good for people to have a place to go that isn't a bar." She looked at me again, as if dying to ask what other problems I needed help with. "It's anonymous you know—just like it says in the name," she said a little regretfully. "Please don't tell anyone that I said Mrs. Baron went there. But, like I said, it's a small town, really, everyone knows."

"And you say Steve married the Baron girl—little Angie— and he cheated on her?"

"Poor baby, I think she started to see through old Steve, and that's why she's on all these antidepressant pills and seeing therapists. It's bound to be depressing."

"Why not get a divorce?"

"Oh, honey, they're strict Catholics. That's a bad word.

A Ton of Trouble

Shhhh. Look!" Bonnie said urgently. She was staring out the plate glass window behind me.

I turned and we both watched two men getting out of a black Mercedes. The driver was the gray-haired man I had seen driving the gray Jaguar on Wolf's property the day of the murder. The man getting out of the passenger seat was the man who had been the passenger in the Jaguar. He was tall and nearly as broad as he was tall, with impassive granite gray eyes and the solid look of a concrete pillar. He was opening the door of the Mercedes with a cautiousness that almost seemed reverent.

The car's driver came around and said something. From the way his taller, broader passenger reacted, it was clear that he took his orders from the older man.

Both men helped a tall, slender, dark-haired woman out of the backseat. She was wearing a black head scarf, dark glasses, black jeans and a blouse—a simple outfit that casually announced itself as expensive.

"That's little Angie," Bonnie said softly, as if they could hear us through the plate glass. "And her dad, Carlo Baron."

Baron stood with his arm around his daughter while the younger man helped another woman from the backseat of the car, she was elderly, judging by the way she moved, but she brusquely gestured to both men to help the younger woman, and she followed behind as the two men supported little Angie across the street as if she were made of hollow eggshells. They pressed a buzzer, spoke into an intercom and were admitted through a dark gray painted door at street level with a brass plaque mounted on it. There was no way to read the plaque from this distance. A moment later the older man came out alone and crossed the street. Bonnie and I stopped and looked at the desk as he came closer and entered the office.

He recognized me immediately. Came over and stood over me, so close that I could smell his bay rum aftershave. Up close his curly gray hair was revealed to be salt and pepper with a lot more salt than pepper. He had heavy, handsome features. Not tall, but he was a heavyset man. "Hi, Mr. Baron," Bonnie said softly.

He nodded, "Bonnie." He looked down at me, standing too close, for effect. "I saw you on the property the other day."

"On Wolf Lambert's property."

"It's really my property, Miss, rightfully mine. I'm Carlo Baron."

"Josephine Fuller." We shook hands.

"You a friend of Wolf Lambert?"

"Yes."

"Ever asked him why he doesn't sell his land to me?"

"As a matter of fact I did."

"Smart lady. What did he say?"

"He said it was his home for the past fifteen years and he's attached to it."

"Tell him he should sell it to me. It's been in my family for over a hundred years. It's only been out of the family the last thirty. You don't want to get in the way of my family, or you could end up getting attached to the land in a real up-close-and-personal way. Will you tell him that for me?"

"I'll tell him what you said."

"That's all I ask. Bonnie, where's Fawn?"

"She's been pretty upset."

He snorted.

"She went home sick," Bonnie concluded.

"Get her on the phone."

"She just left, she probably won't be home for ten or fifteen minutes."

"Keep trying. Transfer the call to my office when you get her." He turned his back and walked into an office that looked out over the street. Just before he closed the door, I heard him say to no one in particular, "I think Fawn needs a vacation—a long vacation."

Bonnie dialed the number. "No answer," she said, and hung up.

"Who was that giant who escorted Mr. Baron's daughter across the street?"

"You're not from round here," Bonnie said with a soft chuckle, followed by a cautious glance at the lit phone light to make sure her boss was still occupied. "That's Jerry Park— he was a football star on the Baronsville High team—a fullback. They used to call him Jurassic Park. Imagine getting tackled by that monster. He should have gotten a college scholarship but—it was tragic."

"What happened?"

"Drugs—some kind of wild party just before graduation. He was in a coma for weeks. He came back physically, but not all the way mentally."

"But I saw Mr. Baron with him in his Jaguar—does he ever drive?"

"Sure. He can drive. He's not that impaired. But Mr. Baron likes to drive when they go out. Little Angie drives her Jag. Jerry drives one of Mr. Baron's other cars when he runs errands. He drives big Angie whenever she goes out, and Carlo's mother, the older Mrs. Baron—you just saw her taking little Angie into her shrink's office. Mrs. Baron is quite elderly.

Anyway, the family paid Jerry's medical expenses and Mr. Baron pretty much adopted him after he came back from the hospital. College, the football scholarship, even junior college was out of the question. I think he's always had a crush on little Angie, but after his accident, the way I hear it, she keeps him away because she doesn't want to hurt his feelings. Poor guy, he clearly adores her, and it's got to be hard seeing her all the time, but he's completely devoted to Mr. Baron. He's so big and scary-looking that he's like a bodyguard, but I couldn't imagine him hurting anyone. He's just sweet and quiet, like a child who's trying hard to act like a grown-up."

I slipped a card into Bonnie's hand. "Call me. I'll buy you lunch."

"Well, I don't know."

"Think about it. Maybe I'll see you at the Lutheran Church."

"I doubt it. It's my daughter who goes there, and the meetings next door aren't at the same time as services." She pocketed the card and picked up the phone and started dialing. This time she reached Fawn. As I walked out, I heard her say, "Mr. Baron wants to talk to you, hon."

As I walked to my car, I took a detour and went to read the brass plate on the door the grieving widow had disappeared through. It read, "Edwina Sarno, M.D., By Appointment Only."

I almost didn't stop at the Blue Movie Store, but I thought
it wouldn't hurt to at least drive by the place. It wasn't far
from 101, and it had an accessible small parking lot next door.
I got out and hesitated outside, looking in the window. I was
surprised. Instead of glossy, in-your-face pictures, the window
was done up in brothel-red velvet with gilt-framed pictures of
the actors whom I guessed must be actors from the videos—
I recognized Thelma and the Manx brothers. There were also
some black-and-white photos and even engravings identified
by labels as Henry Miller, Anaïs Nin, the Marquis de Sade,
and a frame around a mirror labeled "Anonymous." I couldn't
help but think that I wouldn't be anonymous long if I used a
credit card.

I went in and was greeted by a man of medium height
with skin the color of milk chocolate, a short Afro haircut and
a twinkle in his eyes. He was carrying a large long-haired
black cat, with tuxedo-style white chest markings. "Hi," he
said as I came in. "Excuse me, while I move Tricky off this
display; he's trying to discount some of the merchandise. Once
he puts a claw mark on it, I have to cut the price."

I said hello to Tricky, who sniffed my outstretched hand
and allowed me to pet him with total aplomb. I was impressed.

Raoul would have hidden until he was totally sure of a visitor's credentials—of course Raoul wasn't really into retail.

I introduced myself to Maurice and he said, "Oh, yes, Wolf Lambert called and said to hold one of Thelma's videos for you. If he hadn't called I would have sold out. It's all this newspaper coverage. Even my rental copies are out now. I've ordered more, but they're being shipped from LA, so they won't arrive till tomorrow or the next day. I saved the last one for you. It's not one of the ones she made with Lambert, it's her first one, *Big, Bad Biker Babes*."

"Wow, I wouldn't want to try saying that three times in a row."

I looked around the store. It was not a large space but there were tiny alcoves devoted to different subjects. One had a sign over it, "Men at Work," and another was entitled "Women Only."

Maurice saw me looking. "I try to provide a little of everything. Thelma and Wolf's videos are in a section at the back called BBWs, and there's a Bears section next to it for the men who like big men."

He brought out a video and shrugged, "Sorry about the cover. The Lambert production videos are much more—uh, artistically designed. I'll put it in a paper bag for you."

I glanced at the cover and saw that that it provided very accurate thumbnail-sized samples of the explicit acts—presumably stills from the film. I blushed and was happy to have it put in the proverbial brown paper wrapper, in this case a small bag with a tasteful Blue Movie Store logo on it.

"So how long have you had the store here?" I asked, hoping to get past the video box art immediately.

"It's been nearly ten years now."

"And you don't have a problem with small-town morality,

even when there's a scandal like this past weekend?"

"Well, the tourist industry is pretty big here. Visitors are interested in California history, and the building next to this one is a bed and breakfast that used to be a hotel during the gold rush, and then during Prohibition there was a famous roadhouse where all kinds of things happened. As a simple smut shop, I'm just offering a very faint echo of the real wild days."

"Do you know Wolf Lambert?"

"He comes in from time to time. He's a local legend. I carry all his films, even the horror films, although they're not adult films, but people are interested because he's one of our celebrities. I don't sell his wine, because I don't have a liquor license. But there's a little boutique attached to the bed and breakfast that sells gift baskets. They have a special Halloween Wolf Lambert Basket, with a mask, a rubber ax, either Lambert's Lair wine or candy, and either a Hanged Man video or any other gift item from the store—that way they can customize the basket according to the person's taste."

"Do Thelma's videos sell well?"

"Better than you might guess, even before the publicity." He sighed, "Some of the latest sales might be morbid curiosity. Usually the large lady videos have their own dedicated following, and these new viewers might just be looking for shock appeal rather than—"

"Sincere admirers of the larger figure."

"Just a guess, judging by the expressions on their faces. I hope you like it."

"Thanks."

"Come back next week and I should have a good supply of the videos she made with Lambert; those are better."

As I walked to the car, I noticed a familiar face staring at me from behind the steering wheel of the burgundy Cadillac that had been following me all day. I walked up to her and knocked on the window. She threw the door open so suddenly that the edge of it caught me on the knee. I swore and backed up.

Raylene Shotwell climbed out of the car and stepped out in a swirl of Shalimar perfume. She was short but radiating anger that seemed to pump her up. She looked up into my face with a fixed intensity. "I know who you are and I know who you work for. I think you're going to suggest to your employer that she give us a handsome grant. I think you're going to personally recommend it."

"All I can say is I'm not done looking into it yet. If it were my decision to make, at this point I'd say that I think you're doing more harm than good. Maybe I'll find something to change my opinion in the next week or so."

"Oh, I think you'll find it wise to change that opinion."

"Why?"

"Because if you don't, I'll tell your employer how you're spending her time to go look for reasons to get that fat whore off of a murder charge."

"I don't even begin to have enough time to tell you all the myriad of ways that you are mistaken." I turned and walked away with a confidence I did not feel. I liked it better when Raylene wasn't talking to me. Either she herself was capable of tracking down my employer, or she must have some people working with her who were resourceful.

I did not look back, but I sensed her eyes on me as I walked back to the rental car. When I started the engine, I risked a glance. She was talking on the cell phone. She watched me drive out of the parking lot, but didn't follow me.

I headed back to San Francisco. Once inside the Pine Street condo, I put the video on top of the television. I went into the kitchenette area and sat at the small table while I called Sedona Yamada. She answered on the first ring. "Look, Sedona," I explained. "I did talk to Thelma and to Wolf Lambert as well. Wolf said he wanted to pay for any investigation. I'm just not sure how much help I can offer."

"Have you had dinner yet?"

"No."

"Let me take you to my favorite restaurant let's start by pooling our information."

Sedona drove us to a deceptively simple looking Japanese restaurant on Buchanan near the Japantown Peace Pagoda. She suggested the tempura, and the batter-fried shrimp and vegetables were light and crispy, with a very tasty dipping sauce. We sat in a quiet alcove and sipped tea.

"Is it the porn films that make you hesitate to help Thelma?" she asked.

"Maybe, to some degree. I have mixed feelings about that."

"I started out sharing your doubts. But can't you, of all people, understand that when a woman Thelma's size makes an adult film, it makes a different kind of statement?"

"You mean because so many people seem to assume that fat people are asexual?"

"Yes."

"But aren't porno films a rather extreme way to make a statement?"

"I wouldn't choose that way myself. But it's not illegal and I don't want to see Thelma framed as a murder suspect because people don't approve of her videos."

"I don't either."

"So will you help us? You said Wolf Lambert is willing to foot the bill for anything you need."

"This sounds like a conspiracy," I joked. "Wolf did say he would finance some investigation. But I can only work on it in my spare time. I'm not going to jeopardize my job for this—Mrs. Madrone's pretty conservative."

"I understand. But we really need your help."

"I'll do what I can."

"That's all we can ask. There was something you were going to tell me before—after I told you about the cocaine."

"Right—it just so happens that I can add to that." I told her about encountering the two men in the Jaguar coming down from the top of the hill on Wolf's property that day, and about meeting Carlo Baron in his real estate office this afternoon.

She nodded solemnly. "At the very least, that complicates things. Which may be useful. At the very most, maybe they're involved."

It wasn't till I got back to Pine Street that I remembered what it was about Alabama that had struck a chord in my memory. I tried to call Sedona, but got her voice mail and didn't leave a message. I might be able to find the answer elsewhere. Time enough to ask later if that didn't prove to be the case.

I got out Raylene Shotwell's flyer and opened up the laptop computer. A search for newspaper articles netted the information that the church operation she and her husband ran in Alabama had come to the attention of the authorities over their sincere but illegal demand that their employees join their church. A lawsuit was enjoined and the businesses had cut back drastically. None of this explained what Raylene Shotwell was doing in San Francisco affiliated with an antiabortion franchise. There were several Internet articles on the Friend in Need group as well. None of the articles mentioned what law firm had prosecuted the case against Raylene Shotwell.

Finally I shut down the computer and called Mulligan in Seattle.

"I just wondered, would you have any idea how one would go about getting a license plate from Alabama traced."

"What have you gotten into now?"

I explained about the woman from the clinic and how she unaccountably turned up in the parking lot at Newburn's Blue Movie Store. Mulligan told me he might have some ideas, and to call him the next day.

The next morning I started the day with a drive up to Baronsville to talk to Wolf. I could look in on some North and East Bay locations of Friend in Need offices on the way back to San Francisco. Walking into Friend in Need sites was getting more and more depressing now that Raylene Shotwell was openly following me. Sometimes she would take a shortcut and meet me there. She had followed me to the Baronsville turnoff. I hadn't seen her after that, but I didn't doubt I'd see her again today.

Sylvia Terhune met me at the door wearing a long-sleeved striped shirt with a heavy sweater over it. She was so gaunt that I could imagine she might get easily chilled and legitimately need the warm clothing. But then again, she might be hiding fresh wounds under the clothing as well.

"Hi, I hope you're feeling better." I tried not to look at the arms of the sweater in the area where I had seen the blood before.

Sylvia blinked at the question. "Oh, yeah. I'm fine," she said in an embarrassed tone. "Wolf is expecting you. We've got muffins."

Wolf greeted me expansively and pointed out that Sylvia had, in fact, baked the blueberry muffins herself. She had disappeared down the hall before I could sample one, but they were very good and the coffee was also excellent.

"How is she?" I asked after she had firmly closed the kitchen door behind her.

"She seems to be okay today," Wolf said. "Her therapist helps a great deal. Having Steve's body discovered here brought back a lot of painful memories. Arthur and I try to let her know how important she is to us, so she won't feel like giving up on things. I hope it's enough." He sighed. "One day at a time, right?"

"That's the best way to do it," I agreed.

Wolf looked at his notes and brightened. "I've got some ideas of where you can start to look into this matter of Steve's death."

"You do know that I'm not a professional at this?" I said, beginning to dread having agreed to try to help.

"Of course not. A professional would have charged much more money," Wolf said with a raffish smile.

"You haven't got the bill yet, so I wouldn't be so sure," I said. I finished my muffin, took a lingering sip of coffee, and picked up my pen. Sitting and taking notes, I realized that Wolf was outlining a full schedule of activities for my investigation.

"You must have been up all night figuring out this stuff," I said, with something less than admiration in my tone.

"I don't sleep that much, anyway. You should stick around some night and find out." He raised his bushy white eyebrows suggestively. All this planning was invigorating him. He began to detail the arrangements he had made for me to spend this weekend flying down to Los Angeles on a chartered light plane to track down the Manx brothers.

"Isn't that going to cost a fortune?"

"My pilot friend, Farley, goes down there all the time. No trouble at all to bring you along."

As I listened, I realized that Wolf had no ongoing projects. He was a director, looking for something or someone to direct. At the moment it was me.

When he had come up with enough work to keep me busy for a few weeks I stopped him. "Wolf I've got to get to my day job. Remember, I told you I can only look into these other things when I can spare a little time—evenings, weekends, that sort of thing."

"Of course, but you've got to take a lunch hour, right? You could take one of these people to lunch and pump them for information then. Let me give you a check for a thousand for expenses."

I took the check, wondering if signing it would end up spelling the end of my work with Mrs. Madrone. "I'll see what I can do." I got up to go before Wolf could invite himself along. I was pretty sure he didn't want to miss a thing. "Today I've still got to go check out several sites for my employer." I started to edge toward the door.

"Would you mind taking this over to my neighbor up on the hill as you're leaving?" He handed me a basket that looked as if it had come from a Little Red Riding Hood fairy tale— complete with checked napkin folded over the contents. The smell of fresh-baked muffins rose from the basket.

"You're sending muffins to the neighbor with the tele- scope, the one who said she saw Thelma near the stacks of barrels, the night the murder was committed?"

"That's the one."

"You know her?"

"Of course, she's my neighbor. Besides she's as old as God; she knows everyone."

I sighed.

"Please don't make me send Sylvia. She's still a little shaky and I don't want her going out alone yet," Wolf said, playing the feminine nurturing card expertly.

I sighed again. " 'Okay, okay, I'll take it."

I drove up to the neighbor's house on a gravel road that was slightly better tended than Wolf's. It was an old farmhouse, but it looked as if it had been modernized. I had already seen the back deck with the infamous telescope from Wolf's property. From the front it looked in good repair and freshly painted. There were no signs of farming or ranching, although there was a thriving vegetable garden on one side of the house. On the other side, where the hill behind the house sloped down, a path hugged the edge, and a low wooden fence appeared to hold the walkway from falling down the hill.

I went round the side of the house—this was a week for backyards. I could see Wolf's neighbor sitting on the back deck. The telescope was not in use, but she had it out and set up. "Hi," I said, "I brought you a basket from Wolf Lambert, your neighbor."

"I know. I saw you leave from over there. I was expecting you. Saw you before, the day that man's body was found."

"Can I come up?" I indicated the steps up to the side of the deck—it was like being invited aboard a ship. "Or would you rather I came through the front?"

"Young lady, you couldn't fit in the front. Come on up."

I ignored what sounded like an extremely crass insult and came cautiously up the stairs.

"Put the basket on the table next to me. My name is Elmira Jones."

"Pleased to meet you, I'm Josephine Fuller." I put out a hand and she shook it solemnly.

Elmira Jones must have been slightly less than five feet tall and probably weighed about ninety pounds. She was dressed in white pants and blouse and wore a Greek fisherman's hat that looked older than she was. Her shaded face behind dark sunglasses revealed that she must be in her eighties.

"I'm ninety-three."

"I was guessing younger."

"Thank you. People always ask. Want to look through the telescope?"

"Thanks." I went up and squinted through the eyepiece. It was set to zero in on Wolf's parking lot around the area where the barrels were stacked. The lens was so powerful that I could read the print on the side of the barrels. "It's a fantastic telescope. How long have you had it?"

"My son bought it for me fifteen years ago. Sometimes I look at the birds. Lots of hawks around here. Little nesting birds are always chasing them away, sometimes in groups, sometimes just one little guy chasing a big old hawk. Keeping them away from their nests, you know. Sometimes I watch the doings down at Wolf's. It beats the soap operas."

"You must have had quite a view when the police were here."

"Oh, yeah. The night before, too. Saw that great big woman who used to work with Wolf, messing around with the barrels.

She had some fellow with her. A big strapping guy."

"Can you see Carlo Baron's place from here?"

"No. He's on the other side of Wolf. Not that he wouldn't like to buy my land as well as Wolf's."

"And your land—was it part of the Baron family's original property?"

"Not in this century. The Baronsville founder, old Caesar Baron, bought up a lot of land around here for speculation and then sold it again. They never farmed it, although they may have ranched cattle on it. My family bought this property and it was a cattle ranch till the 1950s. There was an apple orchard, but never grapes."

"You've lived here ninety some years."

"Born and raised."

"You must know everything about the area."

The frail old woman looked at me from behind her sunglasses. "What do you want to know?"

"Why does Carlo Baron want the land?"

"Greed, I guess. I'll be charitable and call it family pride. He seems to be pretty sure he can get Wolf's property, and this place is next."

"How long has Carlo Baron been trying to buy back all his family's land?"

"He's been at it for about ten years—with some success."

"When did the father lose it?"

"Come in the kitchen, I'll look in my archives. You can bring the basket. Put it on the table. I'll unpack it later."

I followed her into the house. She took off her hat and sunglasses. Once my eyes adjusted to the dimness, I stood back in awe. I realized what she had meant about my not fitting through the front. Most of the space was stacked with newspapers up to about my shoulder height, which I realized was probably as high as Elmira Jones could reach. Except for an area around the kitchen table, stove, and in front of the cupboards, all the floor space was occupied. The stacks continued down what had once been a hallway, which was now a small passageway with just enough room for Elmira to sidle past.

"Oh, you're shocked. Most people are. That's why I have them come in the back. Hardly anyone could fit in the front part of the place now. I've been collecting this stuff for decades."

"I see." I hardly knew what I was saying. I looked at her, seeming even smaller without the hat, her pink scalp showing through her thinning silver hair. "Uh, have you ever considered getting someone in to help you, uh—" I stopped, totally unable to imagine what could be done about clutter of this magnitude. I have a clutter problem myself, but it was microscopic compared to this.

Elmira seemed oblivious to my reaction. "Oh, I'll have someone in all right. After I die. I'm willing this archive to my alma mater—in fact they will also get the land. Everything. My son understands. He's doing quite well as an orthodontist. He doesn't need it. The minute I go, the Colterville Teachers College gets the whole thing—but only if they catalog and preserve every scrap of paper in the house."

"I'm sure they'll do that." For the kind of property she had, on a hill in the wine country, I was sure it was worth the full-time efforts of a pack of graduate students for a summer copying everything in the small house down to the last label on the last pickle jar.

"You see my point, I'm sure." The old lady said complacently. "I've had a lot of offers on this property. Carlo Baron offered me two million dollars. But what would I do with two million dollars at my age? I've got roots here. I'll go when they drag me out—with any luck that will be feet first. Carlo wasn't happy about it, but it's in his interest to keep me alive in case I change my mind."

"Interesting that you say Carlo has an interest in keeping you alive. Do you think he might be tempted to shorten someone's life span."

"Sit down, honey. Have a glass of lemonade. You can get me some, too. It's in the fridge."

I found the lemonade and a couple of glasses and poured some.

"So Baron wants to buy all this land back?"

"Yes. Carlo Baron—grandson of old Caesar Baron who founded the town. Back in the 1920s, Baron owned most of the property in town. Prohibition was good to him. The Italian and Swiss families in this area were permitted to continue making wine for their personal and religious use, but old Baron Baron, as they used to call him, went into bootlegging and made a fortune. Unfortunately he had a son with a gambling problem and by the late 1970s, most of the old Baron winery land had been sold off. Carlo is a good manager and he's been slowly buying it back. That is admirable. But I simply don't want to sell."

She stood up and began to worm her way into the passageway between stacks of paper. "I'll find that information for you in just a moment, dear."

I realized I could never have gotten through to rescue her if she came to grief in there. "Please don't trouble yourself if it's hard to find."

"Give me a minute to not find it before you start telling me to stop trying. Honest to God people can't sit still for two seconds." A rustling sound came from the next room, and the stack nearest the door tilted alarmingly as Elmira Jones emerged with a couple of sheets of newsprint in her hand.

One was a report dated July 1978, in a local newspaper that Gino Baron, son of Caesar, the founder of Baronsville, had died in Las Vegas of a gunshot wound. Police suspected suicide and cited depression over continuing financial reversals.

While I was reading and taking a few notes, Elmira was eyeing the walls of paper, and she reached out and extracted a magazine from the middle of an unlikely looking tottering stack near the window. "Here it is. BARON REAL ESTATE IN BARONSVILLE—A FAMILY-RUN BUSINESS, it has a picture of that guy who was murdered, the son-in-law."

"May I borrow this? I'll just make some copies and bring it back."

"You may borrow it. But I would like it back."

"Absolutely."

As I was carefully tucking the pages into a plastic sleeve in my notebook, Elmira casually asked, "Did you know there's a blond woman in a wine red Cadillac following you?"

"Yes, I know about that one. She's hard to miss."

"Did you know while you were visiting Wolf, she parked on the frontage road and drew a bead on your car with a very large rifle? I'd say it was for deer, maybe a thirty-ought-six. She had it trained on you the whole time you were standing in the doorway talking to that housekeeper who works for Wolf. I'll bet she had shooting lessons when she was a girl. Probably an only child. Sometimes they get special treatment and sometimes it's not so good."

"Thank you for the basket." Elmira lifted the red-and-white-checked napkin and extracted a foil-wrapped packet that was nestled among the blueberry muffins. "This is my medical marijuana. Wolf was so nice to send me some."

"WHAT?" I stared at the old lady, who was happily open-ing the tinfoil and sniffing its contents.

"Oh, I need it for my glaucoma. I have a prescription, but it's hell getting it. Some of my neighbors who sometimes get hold of a little send it my way, and it's much appreciated, let me tell you."

I could scarcely make my good-byes coherent, I was so angry at Wolf. I slammed the car door and started the engine, already rehearsing a few choice words for Wolf. Just what I needed. To be arrested for carrying drugs to a woman who might be testifying against the man who was furnishing the drugs. I made up my mind I was going to tell Wolf what he could do with his so-called investigating job.

But before I could get back to Wolf's property, my cell phone rang.

It was Bonnie from the realty office. She was crying.

"Were you serious about taking me to lunch?"

"Of course. When would you like to go?"

"How about right now?"

I looked at my watch. It was nearly 12:00. "Where shall I meet you?"

So shoot me, I'm curious. No, I take that back, after all that talk about deer-hunting rifles, don't shoot me.

I looked around for any sign of a red Cadillac and didn't see it. Maybe Raylene Shotwell had given up. Either that or she was up in the bushes somewhere with her rifle.

I picked Bonnie up in downtown Baronsville on a corner a few blocks away from the realty office. Her fine-drawn face was blank, but when she got into the car I could see she was shaking with emotion. But not until she started giving me directions did I realize she was furious.

A few minutes later we pulled into the parking lot of a diner just outside of town. The room was packed, with the five or six wooden tables placed along the length of the wall full of lunchtime diners. Bonnie nodded to the waitress behind the counter and led the way back to an outdoor dining area that was a little more rustic. For some reason no one was out here. The waitress brought out plastic-coated menus, "The burgers are good here, and the tuna melts—I wouldn't advise the chili, though," Bonnie said, as much to the waitress as to me. I went with the tuna melt and Bonnie ordered a cheeseburger and two bottles of beer. "Just coffee for me."

"That's two bottles for me," Bonnie looked at me challengingly. The waitress waited.

"Okay, no problem, two bottles of beer for you. One cup of coffee for me."

"Don't want to get in Bonnie's way." The waitress winked at me as she left.

"I take it you know the waitress."

"She's my cousin. But she's okay."

"What happened?" The waitress arrived with a tray bearing two chilled bottles of beer, a glass, a cup and saucer, and a pot of coffee. She opened the beer and poured it into the glass, put the second bottle next to the first, poured me a cup of coffee, and departed.

Bonnie drank half the bottle of beer and sighed. "Mr. Baron fired Fawn."

"You mean because of the affair with Steve?"

"I don't know. Maybe. Mr. Baron must have known about it for a long time. Fawn was anything but discreet, and Steve didn't seem to care who knew it. But no one did anything about it till Steve was dead. Mr. Baron told me to take her stuff to her at home because he didn't want her coming back into the office ever again."

"Wow!"

"Wow, doesn't even cover it. They weren't going to tell her where the funeral is. She was in love with the guy—God knows why, he wasn't worth spitting on. But they thought he was handsome, his wife—uh, little Angie, and Fawn."

"I never saw much of him." I didn't mention that I had never seen him alive. In fact, even dead, I had seen just the top of his head. "You must have known him. What was he like?"

"What can I say? Scum rises. I used to call him the baby scumlord. Oh, not to his face. But he was so proud of being cruel. He used to think it was cute to tell stories about how old man Baron used to run flophouses and when the derelicts that lived there couldn't pay, he would throw them out with his bare hands. You got the feeling little Steverino was really itching to be able to throw someone out—and not get charged with assault for it. There was this one tenant that we had, a lady who was dying of cancer, and he boasted that he sent a process server to give her the eviction papers while she was in the hospital."

"He was proud of it?"

"Oh, he told that story to everyone. He said having her in the hospital made it easy to know where she could be reached to serve the papers. That kind of thing made him feel like some sort of ruthless tycoon. He was always making a big deal out of how much power he had. He decided to pay the receptionist twice as much as the bookkeeper. I don't blame Fawn, but was he crazy? Did he think I wouldn't see? I write the checks. When he started taking apartments and even some houses out of the rental base so he could use them for his little fling, did he think no one noticed?"

"Let me get this straight. He was cheating on the boss's daughter with the receptionist in the boss's office, paying the receptionist an exorbitant salary, and using company property as a free love nest?"

"Yup. You know how the whole office found out he was using the properties? One of the guys. Now that's a statement in itself. There's usually a male code of silence about that stuff. Did he think he was so damn powerful that he could cheat everyone and no one would bust him on it? Either he thought that, or else he thought people liked him and would cover for him. Stupid man. Mr. Baron found out."

"What did Mr. Baron do?"

"He said he would have to talk to the kid. That was exactly how he put it 'the kid'—Steve was in his thirties. I missed a couple of weeks in the office because old Steve decided I was responsible for telling Mr. Baron and he got me laid off. If he thought I wouldn't sue, he had another think coming."

"Did you sue?"

"I called the old man and told him exactly what happened. Said I hoped it wouldn't come to a lawsuit. They decided to give me a few weeks off with pay. Then I went back to work just like nothing happened. Steve ignored me, but he tried to make sure I got all the shit work. At least I won't have to worry about any more awkward scenes with him."

"Guess not. Aside from cheating on his wife and his father-in-law, were you the only person he treated badly?"

"Oh, Steverino was an equal-opportunity dirtbag. He only had two skills—lying and stealing. He kissed up to anyone with power and walked all over everyone he considered beneath him. He was such an egomaniac, he expected people to be grateful when he stepped on them. Well, I'm grateful he's dead."

"It doesn't sound like much of a loss. Was there anyone in particular he had quarreled with recently?"

"Oh, he wasn't bothering to do that anymore. He found himself a little toady assistant to do it all for him. Monty Johns adored Steverino. He believed all that crap Steve fed him about how they were the marauding Vikings who were going to pillage and rape and become millionaires. Except Monty got to deal with all the angry contractors Steve shortchanged, and the tenants he ripped off. I don't know what Monty got out of it, but he's inconsolable. He hasn't even been to work since Steve's death. If you ask me, he's taking it harder than Angie."

"Did, um, little Angie know?"

"I don't know. Little Angie's hard to reach. She's always been given everything she ever wanted. Maybe it didn't register that Steve was neglecting her, because her parents made it so easy for her to get whatever she wanted without even telling Steve. Maybe she wrote him off. If he'd been my husband, I would have hung him out to dry. But she was raised a strict Catholic. Maybe she really does believe until death do us part."

"I guess death parted them."

"Lucky for her."

"You wouldn't happen to have Monty's address, would you?"

She snapped open her address book and gave it to me. After lunch she asked me to drop her at Fawn's house. "I'll call my husband to come get me," she said. "Meantime, I'll hold Fawn's hand. No one else is bothering to do that."

Monty Johns lived in a small, square house that greatly resembled a house trailer in Rohnert Park, half an hour's drive from the real estate office in Baronsville. There was no answer, but I heard music cranked up very loud, coming from the backyard. I recognized Tchaikovsky, *Swan Lake* act 2, scene 1.

I particularly liked that music, and I hoped Monty wasn't about to spoil it for me forever. I went through the gate of a white picket fence into the backyard and came upon a thin blond man in his forties, sitting in a lawn chair, with his feet up and a cooler of canned margaritas by his side. He was contemplating his neighbor's high, wooden fence and sipping from a plastic cup. A trash can next to him held a pile of empty margarita cans. That made me think of the mysterious piña colada mix on the table with all the sex toys.

When he heard the gate creak, Johns jerked in his chair, as if an electric shock had gone through him. He stared at me wildly. "What do you want?"

"I just want to talk to you."

"Please don't hurt me. I didn't know. I never knew anything he was doing."

"Then what are you afraid of?"

He looked at me blearily. Whatever he was expecting, he was starting to get that I wasn't it. "You're not from him are you?"

"Mr. Johns."

"Yeah."

"Are you okay?"

"No. Who are you?"

I introduced myself and said I had got his address from someone in the Baron Real Estate Office.

"After what happened to Steve Farquar, I just want to make sure you were okay."

"How could I possibly be okay after what happened to Steve?"

"You sound like you're expecting it to happen to you."

A shade of concern passed over his face like a shadow. "I keep expecting to see that big moose of a bodyguard."

"Jerry Park? I thought he was harmless."

"Let's just put it this way. He follows Mr. Baron's instructions. If Mr. Baron told him to break your arm or your neck, he wouldn't even hesitate."

"How do you know that?"

"I've never seen him be violent, but you hear things." He took a long shaky breath. "You're right though, Mr. Baron wouldn't have sent you. Who did send you?"

"May I sit down?"

"You didn't say who sent you."

"I just want to ask a couple of questions, because so far you're the only person I've met, with the possible exception of Fawn, who seems to have liked Steve."

" 'With the possible exception of Fawn,' that's rich." Monty drained the last of the margarita can into his glass, drank it down, tossed the can into the trash, and opened a new can. "I can't say I liked him, but if I hadn't done what he said, he would have got me fired. Then after I'd done what he asked for a while, he told me he could get me fired on a whim because he'd been keeping track of how I'd been skating close to the law. Sometimes over the line. Bastard. You're right. Fawn wasn't the only one stupid enough to believe she could ride his coattails to glory."

"I was over in the office yesterday and it looked like Carlo Baron was firing Fawn. He's afraid she'll show up at the funeral, so he's trying to make sure no one tells her where it is."

Monty snorted with laughter, "The funeral." He upended the rest of the margarita can into his glass. The empty can joined its sisters in the trash. "By the time of the funeral, I'll be so out of here. Why would she want to go? Oh, right she's playing the wounded mistress—the woman he really loved."

Monty snickered. He was rapidly losing focus here, and I decided to try to get some information out of him before he passed out totally. "What about you? You haven't lost your job, have you?"

"Not yet. But why wait? By the time Carlo Baron finds those books and figures out how Steve was stealing from him, I'm going to be long gone."

An explosion somewhere nearby made us both jump, and the ice bucket on the table next to him flew into the air and hit the side of the house, with ice and margarita cans raining down right and left. It was rifle fire.

Both of us screamed. I saw Monty sprawl full-length down on the grass and thought for a moment he had been shot. Then I realized he was crawling along the lawn toward the shelter of the bushes. I wasn't at all blasé about getting shot at. I followed Monty's lead and moved faster than I would have thought possible on my hands and knees. Another shot rang out and a bullet hit the wall of his house. It was low enough that for one horrible moment I wondered if whoever was shooting could see clearly enough to aim for us on the ground.

We made it to the bushes as another shot hit the trash basket full of empty margarita cans and blew the contents all over the backyard. Crouching in the bushes Monty began to shake violently. Neighbors' heads started popping out of back doors and then popping back in again when another shot rang out and knocked over the lawn chair where Monty had been sitting.

"Was that gun fire?" someone asked from the yard next door.

I heard a car engine starting and someone driving away. Bravely or foolishly, I went around the side of the house to see if it was a burgundy Cadillac with a blond driver. But whoever it was had turned a corner and driven out of sight. I went back to the backyard to retrieve my purse and found that Monty had disappeared. Looking at the back door, I could hear him locking it from inside.

My hands were shaking on the steering wheel as I drove back to San Francisco.

26

As I parked in the parking garage on Pine Street, I realized that I hadn't visited even one East Bay Friend in Need Center. I continued on up to the corporate condo. Once I closed the door, I took a deep breath and sat down on the sofa. Then I stood back up. Too much adrenaline.

I decided to take an unofficial sick day. Perhaps a mental health day in honor of my insanity for deciding to help Thelma and work with Wolf Lambert. I called Mulligan, pacing up and down nervously. He was not in. It was that kind of day.

I wasn't keen on going outside, and I was too wound up to make a lot of sense, so I sat down and typed out a few notes to come to terms with what had just happened to me.

It was more likely to be connected to the Friend in Need Center than to my inquiries for Wolf. If it proved not to have anything to do with them, I might take that part out rather than put it in the final report to Mrs. Madrone. Then again, I might leave it in.

Finally I calmed down enough to be able to look at the paperwork I had accumulated on various offices of the counseling service that I had visited so far. Allowing for the different communities, the centers were basically identical, and they all seemed to know Raylene Shotwell. I could make a case for not visiting the others and finding another way to get information. The next step would be to talk to some women who had been counseled by the service.

I had accumulated a couple of names from clients and former clients of the organization who had said they wouldn't mind talking to me. I began to call. Once they realized why I was calling, the women's reactions varied widely.

The first woman was very earnest: "I was saved from a terrible mortal sin by talking to those women." She proceeded to ask if I was interested in attending Sunday worship services and I declined politely.

The next woman was really angry: "They advertise in the Yellow Pages as offering a full range of family-planning services," she said, "but all they really wanted to do was talk me out of getting an abortion. I asked if they offered contraceptives, and they told me abstaining from sex was the only way. I slammed the door on the way out and went over to Planned Parenthood."

The third woman I talked to asked if we could meet to talk in person. "I could buy you some coffee," I offered.

"Make it a hamburger and I'll be there," she said, laughing.

The address she gave me turned out to be a fast-food place just a few blocks away from the Friend in Need offices. The woman I met, who identified herself only as "Frieda," was short, red-haired, and freckled. She wore no makeup and was dressed in jeans and a white sweatshirt with a sentence on it in small print.

We went into the restaurant together and stared at the illuminated menu above the counter, with pictures and prices. Frieda looked at me questioningly.

I told her to order anything she wanted and she deliberated over the menu, glancing at me again shyly as she finally ordered the largest double cheeseburger on the menu, double fries, and a strawberry milkshake. I had orange juice and a fish sandwich.

We sat inside. There were enough unsavory characters walking past the window to make me nervous but Frieda didn't seem to notice them. While we ate our fast food I couldn't help but look again at her T-shirt. Up close I could read the words on it: BREAST MILK, AFFORDABLE HEALTH CARE.

"Um, do you have any problems wearing a T-shirt like that—particularly in a rough neighborhood like this?"

"No. Why should I?"

I sighed, suspecting a case of terminal naïveté. "Uh, don't some men, uh—"

"It's not aimed at men," she said patiently, as if explaining to a particularly slow child. "It's to encourage more women to breast-feed."

"Aha. I see."

We ate in silence until only a few french fries were left. Then she sighed. "What do you want to know about the Friend in Need Center?"

"How did you hear of it?"

"Unfortunately, I never used the center's services."

"Unfortunately?"

"I've never been pregnant. Can't get pregnant. I've always wanted a baby, but God had other plans. I can't work, I've got a chronic illness. The medication I'm on—it wouldn't be wise to have a baby even if I could—which I can't."

"I'm so sorry."

"As long as I take my pills, I'm okay. I've been volunteering at the center ever since it opened here in San Francisco. Before that I volunteered other places, but the center makes it possible for me to help young women in trouble and also to help couples who are looking to adopt. We do good work. Some people don't believe that, but we do."

"What do you say when women come in and ask about abortions?"

"I beg them to reconsider. There are couples desperately wanting to love those babies. It won't be easy to spend nine months carrying a child and then turn it over to someone else. But it will be the right thing."

"What if a woman is bound and determined to get an abortion?"

"We don't physically stop her, of course. We do encourage her to come back if she needs to talk afterward."

"I've heard that people from your organization get together to stand outside Planned Parenthood clinics to intimidate women who might be getting abortions or even getting contraception."

"I don't do that."

"And your organization doesn't offer any contraceptive services or advice other than to abstain from sex."

"That's true."

"Why not?"

"Other places offer that. We don't believe in it, why should we help them do what we think is wrong?"

"Would you mind if I called you if I have any other questions?"

"Of course not." She gave me a couple of phone numbers, one of which was for the center itself.

That gave me the idea to talk to some of the other centers in town that offered similar services to see what they had to say, but that would have to wait till tomorrow. Maybe before I flew down to Los Angeles.

I called Mulligan. He had just arrived home. He told me
he was stretched out in an easy chair with two cats in his lap.
I tried to imagine that and it cheered me up a little. I found
myself telling him about my encounter with Raylene Shotwell
and the scene at Monty Johns's place.

"Someone was shooting at you?"

"At me and or at Monty Johns."

"Tell me again who this guy Monty is."

"He's a coworker of the man who was killed. Evidently
they were doing some kind of skimming operation from the
Baronsville's real estate office and Steve was setting Monty up
to take the fall."

"So the possible shooters are the crazy lady in the Cadillac
and someone who is angry at this Monty character?"

"Yes. Those are ones I can think of so far. You don't really
sound too surprised that someone was shooting at me."

"There's not much I can do about it from here. But maybe
you should give her a taste of her own medicine."

"What, shoot at her?"

"No. You're not even sure it was Raylene who shot at you,
right?

"Not totally sure, no."

"Call Dowd and Ramos."

"Who?"

"Harvey Dowd and Wally Ramos—the guys you met at
the convention. Come on, Jo, it was only a few days ago."

"Right. The bad news bears." He laughed at that description. "Sorry, Mulligan, something about being with you drives
all thoughts of other men from my mind."

"Yeah, right. That's why you're hanging out with some
dirty old man who makes porno movies. They're licensed PIs,

A Ton of Trouble

Jo. Tell them to put it on my tab and find out what Mrs. Raylene Shotwell is hiding."

"Are you sure she's hiding something?"

"If she's breathing and over twenty-one, she's hiding something."

"I had no idea you were so cynical."

"It's the cats. Their natural predatory ways are rubbing off on me."

The conversation deteriorated after that and I hung up the telephone thoroughly warmed and only a little stirred up. I had Harvey and Wally's local number on the notepad by the telephone. I decided to wait until the next morning to call it.

The next morning I was awakened by a loud buzzing. It took me a few moments to realize that it was the intercom to the outside door. Evidently the security guard was not on duty. It wasn't even 8:00 A.M. and I had to ask twice who was there. I buzzed them in and hurried to throw on a flannel shirt and pants before the hallway door sounded a similarly annoying buzz. I opened the door to Harvey Dowd and Wally Ramos.

"You're up early," I said, rubbing my eyes and going to run water into the coffee maker.

"Mulligan called," Harvey said. He was holding a pink box of doughnuts.

"Really we haven't been to bed, yet," Wally said.

"Want some coffee?"

They both said sure and sat down at the small table next to the kitchenette. They both appeared sober, but I made the coffee strong for my own sake as well as theirs.

"Tell us about this religious nut who's following you," Harvey said, as I poured the coffee. I held up a hand, fixed my coffee and took the all-important first few sips before going to get my notes. I read off what I knew about Raylene Shotwell. Both men surprised me by taking notes. The doughnuts vanished rapidly.

When I had finished, my coffee was also gone. I asked them if they wanted more.

"No," Harvey said, "I think we want to get started. It's nearly noon on the East Coast, and that's where we've got to call. We've got a bet on with Mulligan who can come up with the dirt on this Holy Roller first. That boyfriend of yours is good, but, honey—" he looked at Wally.

"We're better," Wally said with a wink.

"Thank you." I felt oddly touched. "Oh, Harvey?"

"What?"

"Here's your camera back. There's a picture of Raylene Shotwell in one of the Friend in Need offices that I took."

"You surveilled her?" Harvey said, in wonderment, taking his camera back.

"No. I just whipped out the camera and took her picture."

The two men exchanged smiles, "It's different," Wally said, "but it could work."

"Let's get going," Harvey said. "Can't let Mulligan down." We shook hands all round. "We'll check in tonight. We should have something by five. I told them I would be in Los Angeles, but gave them my cell phone number. I was comforted knowing that they might be able to come up with something to stop Raylene before she decided to start shooting again.

T he next morning I met Wolf's pilot friend, Farley, at the Santa Rosa airport. He was a tall, heavyset man in his late forties with a Neanderthal eyebrow overhang. He gruffly admitted that he was scheduled to fly into Van Nuys Airport in the San Fernando Valley. "I told Wolf I'd drive you to the factory." He looked me up and down and shook his head, "You sure you want to do that? I mean go there?"

"Wolf said they would know where to find the Manx brothers."

"Yeah." He threw his Styrofoam cup still half full of coffee into a trash can. "Those guys move around a lot." He led the way out to the airplane and even helped me climb into it and strap on the seat belt.

The day was overcast, but Farley explained that it wasn't a problem for flying. My anxiety cheered him up a bit and he demonstrated his skill with the airplane to put me at ease. Once we were airborne, he cheered up even more. It was clear that he really loved flying. I didn't want to distract him. The small plane was noisy enough that real conversation would have been a strain. From time to time I asked a question about the instruments or the route and he answered at length. After a pit stop for gas at a small airfield in the San Joaquin Valley, he landed the plane without incident at Van Nuys and led the way to his car, which was a rather battered white Jaguar. I was impressed.

"I keep the car here because I fly in so much."

"How about this factory? Is it hard to find?"

"It's just a factory in North Hollywood. I've been there before. They've got minimum-wage workers putting the cassettes together, and they do some editing on the premises, too. The Valley is the capital of the porno business."

"Why is that?"

He looked at me as if I were crazy. "It's the entertainment capital of the world. They use the same techniques and some of the same talent to make porno that they do to make straight videos."

The front door of a nondescript warehouse led into a warren of small offices. A stocky young person with a shaved head and so many facial piercings that I felt like counting them was talking to a brunette in very tight denim cutoffs and a croptop T-shirt. The brunette's breasts were so out of scale with the rest of her body that it was hard to look anywhere else. When she turned to face us, I was startled to see that her face looked bruised.

"What happened?" I asked, assuming a traffic accident or something of the sort.

"I just had my nose and lips done," she said with a sorelipped smile.

"I thought you were perfect the way you were," said the very pierced person, whose voice indicated she was female.

Both women greeted Farley by name, but I thought I detected a note of caution in their voices.

"This is Josephine Fuller," Farley said. "She needs to talk to the Manx brothers."

"You better ask Hymie. He's back in the factory."

We went down a maze of cubicles to a back office at the edge of a large factory floor, where the actual videocassettes were being assembled.

Farley introduced Hymie—I amended that to Jaime when I realized he was Latino—a man in his fifties with a sour expression and eyes like flat black paint. He had been editing a video on a computer workstation. He froze it to talk to us. A close-up of pink flesh.

"The Manx brothers. Yeah, they were here yesterday. And now they're not. Why should I tell you anything?"

"As a favor to Wolf Lambert."

"Oh, yeah, you're his kind of girl. I heard that about him."

"You want me to call him?"

"Suit yourself."

I opened the cell phone and pressed a button, grateful that I had thought to put Wolf on the speed dial. He answered and I told him where I was and who I was talking to.

"Let me speak to him."

Whatever Wolf said to Jaime produced an instant change in him from sneering to sulking. He said, "Yeah," a couple of times and then folded up the phone and handed it to me. "The Manx brothers are at Sam Delano's in Lizard City, about an hour's drive outside of Lone Pine."

"I know where it is. Sam Delano's got his own landing strip," Farley said. "I was at Sam's party there Labor Day—"

"Who wasn't?" Jaime said snidely. "Sam's got some hot new talent over from San Diego. The Manxes are doing a weekend shoot." He turned back to his editing console. I had already ceased to exist.

I took a moment to use the rest room and found the woman in cutoffs and the highly pierced woman had taken refuge in there and were sharing a hand-rolled smoke of highly questionable legality.

"Say hi to my girlfriend, Ivy, in Lizard City," the pierced woman said, "She's the AD—that's assistant director—on that film."

"And watch out for Farley. Did he do his famous copping a feel in midair stunt?" the brunette asked.

"So far no," I said.

"Oh, he won't bother her, he doesn't like big girls."

"He was all over me when he took me up in his plane. I thought we were going to crash."

"Well, no one could resist you, sweetie."

"This was before the implants."

"You were just as hot back then."

Farley and I headed for the car, the airport, and Lizard City.

On the way to the airport Farley described how to get to Lizard City by road—a process that evidently took about five hours driving from Los Angeles.

Once we were airborne in the small plane we didn't talk much, but I was glad not to be driving through the dusty, arid landscape below. The airstrip behind Sam Delano's house looked like a rut in the desert, with a spectacular view of the Sierras across a totally flat vista of desert and scrub. Farley pointed out that even if we went off the strip, the desert and scrub were more forgiving than some places he had landed. Then he fell silent and concentrated on bringing the plane down, which he did perfectly. I told him as much, and he seemed gratified. The prospect of spending a great deal of time in a desert stronghold with the Manx brothers and a bunch of sun-baked swinging porn moviemakers did not thrill me wildly. Farley on the other hand was brightening up considerably at the chance of voyeurism at the very least, and possibly more. If we did end up staying longer than I wanted, no doubt he would be in a very happy mood.

It was late afternoon in Lizard City and still ninety degrees of dry desert heat. The hill where Sam Delano lived provided a view of the entire town—a former mining-company town, now shrunk to one main street with a couple of house trailers and a few shabby buildings.

"No one appears to have noticed the plane landing," I said to Farley.

"Some of the people in Lizard City don't much like Sam—either they disapprove of his lifestyle, or they're jealous, or they're just weird. The desert's a mind-your-own-business kind of place. Over in Death Valley, Charles Manson and his gang used to ride their dune buggies and hatch their crazy plans. The local people knew they were bonkers, but it wasn't their business. It's like that with Sam shooting his porno movies. It's nobody's business."

Farley led the way along a short dirt road through the creosote, scrub brush, and prickly pear cactus to the house. A couple of Jeeps and two vans were parked nosed up to a concrete block fence a few feet from the wall of the house. Farley didn't even knock.

Shooting must have concluded for the day because the cast and technicians were all lounging around in shorts and T-shirts in a darkened living room, eating chips and dip and drinking beer and wine. I recognized one woman from the scene where Thelma's video was almost shot—she was the one who told me piña colada was their secret weapon. I waved, and she came over and shook my hand. "I'm Ivy, the assistant director," she said, no doubt taking pity on my dazed look.

"I remember you from Thelma's but we weren't properly introduced."

"Yeah, it was a little chaotic."

"I've got to talk to the Manx brothers."

She wrinkled her nose in distaste, but gestured to where

A Ton of Trouble

two men lounged on a sofa near the refreshment table. "I'll leave you to it. There's refreshments there. Help yourself."

I noticed that Farley stayed away from Ivy. But he was staring at two blondes with deep tans and breasts that appeared to need their own zip codes, pressing up against thin T-shirts. I blushed and looked away, realizing they weren't wearing anything but the T-shirts as they stood in the doorway that led back to a kitchen, returning Farley's shares with encouraging giggles.

The room smelled of sweat, sex, and pot smoke. An X-rated video was playing with the sound turned down. For some bizarre reason, that reminded me of a waiter I knew who told me the staff at his place of employment would usually adjourn to another restaurant after the day's work was over. Busman's holiday.

Farley gestured me over brusquely and introduced me to Sam, the director, a stocky man with the trendy haven't-shaved-in-a-week look that constrasted with his baldness in a bad way. He said hello and companionably offered food and drink. I took a glass of wine and looked at the rest, realizing that although I hadn't eaten since breakfast, I was more queasy than hungry. The place was making the hair raise up on the back of my neck. For a moment I realized I was the largest person in the room—except for Farley.

Having done his duty, Farley had gravitated into the kitchen to chat with the two blondes. They had removed their T-shirts, and through the open door, I could see that one of them was using a face towel and a pump bottle of soap to scrub makeup off her naked breasts at the kitchen sink. The other girl joined her, and they began comparing recent implant scars. Farley appeared to be an expert on the subject, and I could tell that he was going to be doing some close examination and holding forth for quite a while on the topic.

I realized I was now on my own getting out of this place. Farley was not going anywhere anytime soon unless someone threw a bucket of cold water on him. For some reason it irritated me even more that I was going to look like a jealous, unattractive bitch if I tried to drag him out in his current horny condition. Farley and I had a cordial, impersonal relationship and I wanted to keep it that way at least until he delivered me safely near a rental car.

I took a deep breath and went up to Rod Manx, "Excuse me, we met at Wolf Lambert's place and again at Thelma's."

"Hi, again."

"I came out here to ask you a couple of questions. It won't take long."

"Take your time. Ringo and I don't usually do fat girls, but if the price is right, we'll do anything."

Ringo smiled. His sunglasses tonight had yellow lenses. "Catch us quick before we get too much wine in us. I think we've still got a little juice, what do you think, Rod?"

Rod smiled. His face was as handsome as ever, but with a few minutes to observe him up close, I could see the twist beneath the smile. "We had a pig contest with one of the other actors. Thelma put us over the top. You know what a pig contest is?"

"I imagine you're going to tell me."

"We compete to see who's screwed the fattest, ugliest girls. We couldn't find anyone who screwed any girl fatter than Thelma—and we both did, so we won that one. I offered to buy her a bottle of wine for helping us win but she told me to shove it, and I told her that would cost her an extra hundred if she wanted to film it—two hundred if Ringo does the shoving."

"We can get it up for anyone—or anything," Ringo said matter-of-factly. After all, he was describing a job skill.

"And you always work together?"

"Yeah. So?"

"You're probably getting it up for each other, then. You don't even need a girl, a boy, or a donkey."

"You're saying we're gay?"

"No, I'm not paying you that kind of compliment."

"You came all this way just to insult us?"

"Wolf Lambert paid for the ticket. It was my idea to ask you if you saw anything at Lambert's Lair—after all, Rod, you were standing right near that stack of barrels where the body was discovered."

They exchanged a lightning-swift glance. Rod folded his arms across his chest. "You found the body. We didn't even see it."

"Yeah, but you saw something. You could tell me about it. You might not even have to talk to the police. Of course, if you don't tell me about it, I'll have to tell the police I'm pretty sure you're hiding something, which is clear. And they'll talk to you."

"We haven't done anything," Rod said.

"But you saw something, didn't you? Something you didn't want to talk to the police about."

"If Lambert doesn't want to work with us, that's his call. I didn't see anything the day we went over there with Thelma. But when we were there before working with Wolf, we saw a guy who has been dealing speed forever." Ringo glanced at his brother.

Rod shrugged. "True."

"What was his name?" I asked.

"Didn't catch his name." Rod caught Ringo's eye and some signal passed between them. "Seen him before, talking to people who sell coke. He walked away when he saw us."

Ringo laughed. "He walked away because we took the girl he was talking to. That receptionist at Wolf's—the little brunette. She wants to get into films. She was talking to that guy, but when we came up, she turned her back on him and came over to ask how to get into movies."

"We never caught the guy's name." Rod got up and took his brother's arm.

"Hey, we never even caught the brunette's name, and she was going to audition with us," Ringo said.

"Is that enough for you?" Rod was walking Ringo out of the room. "That's all we saw. Really Ringo saw it and told me, I didn't even notice."

I moved closer to Ringo, "What did this drug dealer look like?"

"Maybe a shade shorter than we are, just under six feet. Light brown hair, real short. Real straight looking. He was wearing business clothes—not a tie, but you know, chinos and short-sleeved shirt with a sport coat. He gave me a card— which I promptly threw away, of course. Something to do with real estate."

"Could his name have been Steve?"

Rod stopped and glared at me. "His name could have been Marco Polo for all we knew. We didn't get the man's name. Okay?" The cold hostility in his eyes now had no veil of geniality over it. "We haven't been at that place since we drove Thelma over the day we met you. She came to get her CDs. She got her music and we left. Now leave us alone."

He pulled his brother from the room and I was left alone with Ivy. Farley was heading toward the back bedroom. "Wait a minute," I started to say, but the door closed behind him and I wasn't about/get near that scene.

"Don't worry about it."

I looked over to see Ivy near the door with her gear piled around her. "Help me carry this out to the Jeep and I'll drop you at the motel in Lone Pine. Unless you want to stay here." She indicated the empty sofa with the television set in front of it, still silently playing the adult video, although no one was now watching it.

Might as well cut Farley some slack," Ivy said as we loaded gear into the van. "He hangs around the porn shoots when he can. You'd think girls would be excited to go with a pilot, but he really comes off as a loser. Two blond porn starlets with boob jobs is an offer he can't refuse."

"You think I'll be able to arrange some alternate transportation from Lone Pine?" I asked as we got into the four-wheeler, which turned out to be a Jeep with a windshield and a roof that appeared to be constructed along the same lines and of the same material as your average tent.

"Sure, if you want, I can drive you back to LA, I'll be heading back to get this video edited tomorrow. If you're in a hurry, you might want to try calling Sam's first. Farley probably won't wake up till noon, anyway, and you don't want him flying you anywhere till he gets his head clear."

"Oh, that reminds me, a woman with about twenty pieces of metal in her face over at the video factory said to say hi. She said she was your girlfriend."

"In her dreams. Well, we had one night, but she's such a kid." Ivy shook her head.

"Thank you."

"For what?"

A Ton of Trouble

"For reminding me of all the disappointments women who date women can have. Sometimes men are such a pain that I imagine that lesbians have it easier."

"Well, there are certain advantages to not having to deal with men, but they're mostly superficial. And unless you go the totally separatist route, you've got to deal with men all the time."

"I would imagine that porn films would be no place to escape."

"Not unless they're girl-on-girl films, I want to do those in the future. But it was easier to get a job with these guys. The pay is good and I need the experience."

"You can put this on your résumé?"

"Sure."

"I might take you up on the ride if I can't get air transport—I don't have a lot of time and Wolf Lambert is paying for the ticket."

"You should be able to get a ride with Farley. Seriously, he's fine once he gets his libido under control."

"How did you get involved in this business?"

"I have a degree in film and it's hard to get work. At least this is experience and it pays the bills. Some of it—the girl-on-girl stuff—I even enjoy." She cast me a cautious look.

"Okay, one thing has been bothering me for days."

"What's that?"

"What was so funny with the piña colada mix?"

She laughed. "That's for the money shot."

"Money shot? Thelma mentioned that. What is it?"

"Let's just say there are some things a man can't fake, particularly not on camera. But if you put water and piña colada mix into a condom, twist and secure the open end, then put a hole in the tip and pinch it off till it's needed. The man holds it concealed in his hand till the time is right, then squeezes and bingo! It looks just like a certain popular male bodily fluid. But it photographs better and it's infinitely more predictable."

"And that's what bothers you?"

"Oh heck, I don't care about it. Of course, we shoot it like it was Niagara Falls."

"Oh." We both started to laugh. "Well, it probably feels like Niagara Falls to them," I guessed.

"Uh-huh." There was a short, amused silence.

"Thelma said she wanted to leave the money shot out, but Wolf convinced her to keep it in. There are some women producers who are making porn aimed at a couples audience and they got holy hell for not even putting in a money shot. It hasn't affected their sales because they know their market. Most women really don't want to see it. See, now with your big-girl videos, like Wolf Lambert and Thelma do, the audience is 99.999 percent male, so there's no getting away from it."

"You're saying that while Thelma's films don't have a female audience, some porn does?"

"That's right. Female audiences want more plot and atmosphere, while male audiences usually trade atmosphere for action. Thelma's films have a very small but dedicated audience of men who like big women. Very few women can watch them. Women are conditioned to get very nervous at the very sight of a bulging tummy."

"When we see a naked woman, we look for her figure flaws."

"True. Even lesbian filmmakers have that conditioning, although we're supposed to be more accepting of different body types, at least when it comes to rhetoric. In practice I think American women are even more screwed up than American men about sex. At least men know what they like. Queer or straight, most women are so brainwashed to worry about how they look or what their partners will think of them, that half the time they can't even pay attention to sex."

I sighed. "I guess it's the same all over."

Ivy sighed, too. "It can be its own particular brand of hell, as I can testify." There was a pause and then she smiled. "I did like the way you busted the Manx brothers in the chops. I've been dying to do it all weekend but I have to keep working with them, so I couldn't."

"My pleasure."

I was able to secure a room at the motel with no problem. I sat down on the bed and thought about what I had learned. I noticed that my message light was blinking on the cell phone. The last thing I was expecting was a message from Monty Johns. After our adventure under fire, I figured he would want to stay away from me.

"I got your number from Bonnie. I want to talk to you. I'm in LA." He left an address in Las Palmas and a number with a 213 area code—Los Angeles. I called it, but it just rang. No answer and no answering machine.

30

Farley responded to an 11:30 phone call the next morning and met me at the Lone Pine Airport looking refreshed. He flew me back to Los Angeles with a minimum of conversation. I explained about the call from Monty, and he agreed to drive me there. The weather was even grayer when we got to LA.

"God, it looks like it's going to rain," I said.

"Maybe we can get out before it does, if this drive doesn't take too long."

But it was already raining when we found the address in Las Palmas, an invisible community in the western part of Los Angeles—one of dozens of places on the map that only lived in the memory of older residents. They had once been small towns. But Greater Los Angeles had strangled them with freeways and eaten them back in the 1950s and '60s. The streets had palm trees and shade trees mingled in together. Old-fashioned single-family homes had mostly given way to apartment complexes of varying sizes, most of them with swimming pools in varying states of cleanliness.

The address Monty had given me was for the second story of a three-story complex of apartments built in the Southern California motel style of architecture, centered around a swim-

ming pool that took up most of the courtyard. We kept under
the shelter of the balconies of the second-story apartments as
the rain drenched the pavement around the pool and began
to collect in the white molded plastic chairs someone had left
at one edge of it. The steps up to the second floor apartments
were already wet. The walkway was deserted. If anyone was
home in any of the apartments, they were being very quiet.
There was a deserted but not abandoned feeling about the
walkway. Monty's apartment door stood wide open.

Farley and I hesitated in the doorway. He seemed more
shocked than I was, but then I had had a rough week and
numbness was setting in.

The apartment had been recently trashed. Broken fixtures
and smashed windows. Glass and pieces of furniture every-
where. The spray-painted graffiti on the walls was not the carefully crafted creation of a tagger. In simple block letters, the
most popular four-letter obscenities were repeated.

I hated to go in there, but if Monty was still there, we had
to see if he was hurt. But there was no sign of life, and thank-
fully no visible signs of damage done to a living creature.
Farley waited for me at the door.

"We've got to talk to the manager."

Farley just looked at me. But he followed me down to the
first-floor apartment with the black and silver metal "Manager"
sign affixed to its door. The woman who answered was in her
twenties, blond, with dark roots growing out and ready to take
over again. She had round brown eyes and stared at us with
the world-weary air of someone who had seen it all and wants
to see less. Two small, grubby children clung to the hem of
her maternity smock. She ran a hand over her face and admitted that there had been some kind of disturbance earlier
in the day. "Someone was yelling and I heard splashing in the

pool about an hour ago. I didn't pay much attention because I got my hands full here." She lowered her gaze to the two children, who stared at us, but didn't budge or utter a word. "Plus, I got morning sickness, you know."

I nodded and I could see Farley nod, too. Neither of us had actually experienced what she was talking about, but we had both heard of it. "I thought maybe some kids were in the pool. I can't go out there every time somebody jumps in, but I do try to yell at them to have an adult. This time before I even got out to look, everything was quiet. And I never heard anything more."

"Well, somebody trashed the apartment. There isn't any sign of the guy that was staying there. Had he been there long or was he staying with someone?"

"I don't know the tenant in there real well. I've only been managing the place for a year and he was there when I moved in. His name was Johnson and he seemed pretty quiet. He might have had guests." She shrugged. She didn't even seem interested in the trashed apartment. "Did you close the door? It locks by itself."

"I think the lock was broken. It looked like someone kicked it in."

"Oh, well. There's no sense going up there, then. If the door is broken, I couldn't lock it, anyway."

Farley and I stared at her. For the first time I was pretty sure we were both thinking exactly the same thing. He turned and went to the edge of the balcony's shelter to look out over the swimming pool. The manager must have read our minds because she said a little defensively, "I'll call the owner. He may want to do something about it."

She was about to close the door, but Farley was suddenly at my elbow, "Jo, look at the pool." His voice was urgent.

A Ton of Trouble

I went to look and as I did I heard the manager's door close firmly. Farley pointed to the pool.

The man's body in the pool was floating facedown next to a child's inflated toy. The rain beat down on him, but I could see a bloody circle on the back of his shirt just below his shoulder blades. The stringy blond hair fanned out around his head gave me the sinking feeling that it was Monty Johns. I turned back to the manager's resolutely shut door and sighed, then stepped back into the shelter of the overhanging balcony and dialed 911.

Farley and I achieved a sort of unity under fire in the next few hours, explaining to skeptical Los Angeles police officers why we had come to see Monty, how I knew him, exactly where we both were last night and this morning. Then we got to do it again for homicide detectives. Eventually they let us go.

It was late afternoon and the rain was pouring down with monsoon force as we walked back to the car. Of course, it being Los Angeles, we hadn't brought umbrellas or rain gear.

"I think we're going to have to wait till this lets up to fly," Farley said. "You want me to drop you off at a motel near the airport."

"Might as well."

"You want to get something to eat first?"

"Might as well."

The night before I couldn't have imagined sharing a meal with Farley, but we found a family-style restaurant and had a nice meal, feeling very cozy being out of the rain and in front of plates of chicken and mashed potatoes. "How did you get to know Wolf?" I asked.

"A friend of a friend hooked us up when he needed transportation. I was a big fan of his horror flicks and we hit it off."

My cell phone rang. "Speak of the devil. It's Wolf," I told Farley.

"So where are you?"

"In LA, it's raining like it's never rained before."

"It's always a surprise in LA, isn't it? So you're not coming back till tomorrow?"

"That's right."

"Could you drive over and see me when you get back? I need your help."

"Okay."

"Could you put Farley on for a minute, babe."

I handed Farley the phone and he listened, then laughed. "Roger, wilco. I'll bring her back safe and sound before noon." He looked at me. "Wolf hung up, did you want to talk to him again?"

"No, that's fine. I should have asked him why he needs to see me before noon?"

"He wants you to drive him to a funeral."

T he rain had subsided to a drizzle by the next morning. Farley picked me up at the motel near the airport at 7:00 A.M. He must have decided he liked me because he brought me a cup of good coffee and a bagel. I'd already had enough coffee to get me functioning, but I was happy to see the bagel, which had cream cheese and was entirely acceptable. It settled my stomach for the flight back to Santa Rosa.

Listening to him chatter about his future flight plans, I could see that Farley had a different sense of distance than most of us. Heading down to the Sea of Cortez or up to Alaska was like a weekend jaunt for him. The farthest he had flown with a buddy was South Africa. He talked about hopping to other countries as blithely as Mrs. Madrone did, but it was clear that for him a great deal of the thrill of travel was physically controlling the airplane.

We got to the Santa Rosa airport earlier than expected. I parted on friendly terms with Farley and exchanged business cards. After all, we were each other's alibi if the Los Angeles Police Department became seriously interested in us for some reason. I picked up my rental car and drove over to Lambert's Lair. A sign over the tasting schedule announced that the winery was closed until further notice due to illness in the family. I was buzzed in and found Wolf sitting on a bench in the sun outside the winery, as if waiting for me to arrive. Perhaps he was.

I gave him the highlights of my trip to Southern California and finding Monty's body in the swimming pool.

"I never heard of Monty Johns or any of Baron's employees at the real estate office," he said. "Carlo used to call me himself until he started sending that young idiot Steve.

"Had you heard anything about Steve dealing cocaine?" I asked.

"Ridiculous, why should he? His father-in-law paid all the bills." Wolf dismissed the idea with a wave of his hand.

I told him what the Manx brothers had said. The part about propositioning Heather got his attention. "Those boys were auditioning my receptionist, huh?" He stood up and paced the length of the bench and back again. "I did the right thing dumping those bozos. All they have to offer is meat appeal, and their combined IQ doesn't equal that of your average pot roast."

"Wolf . . ."

"I don't expect porn stars to be rocket scientists, but a little self-preservation would be nice." Wolf was still pacing—he didn't look shaky now. The effects of Antabuse and alcohol appeared to have worn off.

"Wolf, I asked a question."

"What dear?" He paused, and came back to stand before me as if just remembering I was there. "Sorry, I was distracted."

"Did you ever hear anything about Steve dealing drugs?"

"No. But then alcohol and women are my downfall, not drugs, so why would I hear about it?"

A Ton of Trouble

"Well, you did manage to come up with that so-called medical marijuana for Elmira Jones."

"Did she say that? I'm sure she was only joking. I would never do such a thing." He spoke solemnly, but I noticed a slight twitching of his mouth. Before I could say anything he reached out and grasped my hand and stood, "My dear, will you come with me now? I need moral support."

"Come with you where?"

"Steve's funeral."

"Come on, Wolf, you shouldn't go there. It's just in bad taste. There will be all kinds of media coverage that you really should avoid. And I'm not about to go there—I don't even know any of the people."

"You can go to give me moral support."

I looked down at the cotton pants and polo shirt I'd worn to fly down to LA. "Look, I'm not dressed to go to a funeral."

"It's a California funeral. The dress code is the least of our worries."

Once I started talking about what I would wear, I had lost the argument. "Why can't Arthur drive you?"

"Shhhh." Wolf lowered his voice. "We're not talking about it, but it was no secret that Arthur hated Steve Farquar. He'll stay here with Sylvia and try to keep her mind off it."

Wolf pulled a cell phone from his breast pocket and pressed a button to speed dial a number. "I'm going now, Arthur. We'll be back for dinner." He turned to me, "You can stay for dinner, can't you?"

The funeral home was an old plaster building with a red tile roof. The parking lot was full but there was some street parking reserved for people going there.

I followed Wolf into the old-fashioned building. The Farquar services were in a large room at the back of the building. We were a little late. I looked at my watch. We couldn't have been more than twenty minutes late. It was so quiet that it took a moment for me to realize from the awkward shuffling of feet that the services were concluding. People were standing in the pews and moving down the aisle to file past the casket and say a few words to the principal mourners up in the first rows.

At the head of the row, I recognized Carlo Baron.

The very large woman on the other side of Carlo, with raven black hair must be his wife, Angela Baron—"big Angie." Bonnie was right, with her raven hair and green eyes she was a spectacular beauty—though many people would not have recognized that because she was supersized—almost as big as Thelma. I had to admire her perfectly tailored black crepe dress. I wanted to ask her the name of her seamstress. Her eyes were guarded and she kept her arm around the whip-thin woman next to her. This must be her daughter.

It was the first time I had seen little Angie up close. She was lovely, but her face had a haunted look that couldn't be explained by recent grief. It must have taken some time and pain to carve those lines into her face. She couldn't have been older than thirty, and she was either numb or sedated because she was simply staring at the floor. Not grieved, not agitated, not even very aware of her surroundings. I was willing to bet that her trip to the psychiatrist in Baronsville had included a tranquilizer prescription.

On the other side of the widow, and patting her other arm, was a very petite woman whose bright white hair even under a minimal hat and veil stood out against the black of her dress. Even her eyeglasses had a chain of jet black beads attached to them. I had last seen her from across the street with her son and Jerry Park, escorting her granddaughter into the psychotherapist's office. Seen up close, her back was slightly bowed with age and no doubt osteoporosis. Carlo's mother would be the widow of the father with the gambling addiction, who had sold off all the land Carlo was slowly buying back. She leaned over and whispered a word or two to her granddaughter.

Baron's constant shadow, Jerry Parks, sat in the row behind the elder Mrs. Baron, although he fidgeted from time to time as if his gray suit didn't fit well. She must have heard his seat creak because the senior Mrs. Baron turned around to look at him and whispered something that made him sit up straight immediately.

There were no other easily identifiable family members. I looked for someone in that group who might be a member of Steve Farquar's family. I recognized Bonnie from the Baron Real Estate Agency. Steve's mistress from the realty company, Fawn, was nowhere in sight. I wondered if anyone had told them about Monty. Perhaps they had received a full report from the person who shot him and threw him in the pool.

"Where's Steve Farquar's family?" I whispered to Wolf.

"No idea," he whispered back. "Maybe he was raised by aliens. That would account for his lack of human qualities. Come on, let's pay our respects." He dragged me up to the front, feeling hopelessly out of place in my white slacks even though I'd thrown a casual sweater over the polo shirt.

Wolf went up to the Barons and murmured a few words to each. Carlo shook his hand with great dignity. I followed along behind him and did likewise, even though Carlo Baron and Jerry Parks both looked at me with a sudden sharpness of focus that made me nervous.

As I grasped Mr. Baron's hand, out of the corner of my

eye I could see Wolf holding Angela Baron's hand with both of his and slipping a folded piece of paper in it. My body actually shielded him from Carlo Baron's view. I wanted to elbow Wolf in the ribs and ask him what the hell he thought he was doing flirting with the mother-in-law of the deceased at a funeral right under the nose of a jealous Italian husband.

By the time I got to big Angie Baron, the paper had disappeared and she took my hand politely. Her eyes met mine briefly when I murmured a few words of sympathy for her loss, then she glanced past me to the woman behind me, who shouldered me out of the way and embraced Angela Baron in a hug.

I took the widow's pale, cold hand in mine and said the first thing that came into my head, which was "I'm so sorry."

She met my gaze. I half expected her to nod in silence but she said very softly, "I'm sorry, too. I wish I had it to do over again."

A firm, wrinkled hand reached out to jerk my hand away, and the elder Mrs. Baron pulled me away from her granddaughter. "So nice of you to come," she said in a tone that would have been more appropriate to the sentiment, "Get out, you scum."

I moved on and followed Wolf past the casket. I wondered if Grandma Baron had seen him pass that note to big Angie. We filed past the casket and I realized it was the first time I had seen Steve's face. When I saw him in the barrel, only the top and back of his head had been visible.

He seemed an ordinary enough man, whom I understood to be in his early thirties. With his eyes closed in death, he seemed much younger, his short brown hair and even features seemed boyish. Angela Baron junior must have found him

A Ton of Trouble

attractive—as had Fawn at the real estate office, and Wolf's secretary.

I followed Wolf down the aisle toward the rear of the room.

"Are you out of your mind?" I whispered, "exchanging notes with someone else's wife at a funeral."

"Don't worry about it." Wolf regarded me without a hint of repentance in his eyes. Sobriety didn't appear to have instilled any common sense in him so far.

There wasn't anyone else Wolf wanted to talk to. Most of the mourners seemed to be local people who knew the Barons. We continued on out to the car where I took a moment to explain to Wolf just how foolhardy I thought his behavior was.

"Totally harmless, dear, although what looks the faintest bit like jealousy is very endearing. I just lent her some videos and I told her she could keep them."

"You mean adult videos?"

He smiled in reply. "She doesn't know just how beautiful she is. It's time someone told her that."

"Wolf! Did you ever stop to think that her husband might have had their son-in-law killed for cheating on their daughter? Did you notice there was no one there who knew Steve Farquar?"

"So you mentioned."

"I wonder if his relatives even know he's dead."

"Maybe it runs in the family. Maybe all his relatives were killed by jealous spouses."

"That's not funny. Think what Carlo Baron would do to you if he thought you were cheating with his wife."

"Angela and I? It was totally innocent, dear." He patted my arm, then squeezed it. "Not like with you—I wondered if you could be corrupted, but Angela is totally innocent. She went straight from virginity to marriage and in recent years to virtual nunhood."

"She's told you that?"

"Between the lines, babe. I simply talked to her over coffee at the meeting room after our twelve-step meetings. We have never exchanged words when there weren't a dozen other people present."

"Oh, wonderful. So you have witnesses that you're chatting up a Mafia wife."

"Settle down. You and I will go to a meeting together next week. I told Angie I would be there. You can go to the OA meeting and talk to her there."

I sighed. There was no derailing him.

"You need to get involved in some other activities, Wolf. I've got to go back to work tomorrow."

"I miss Thelma," he said, out of nowhere.

"How long since you've talked to her?"

"We talk every day, but I haven't seen her in weeks."

"Why don't you call her and ask her to dinner? We can swing by and pick her up if she's free."

"Excellent idea!" He snapped open his cell phone and dialed.

Thelma agreed to come and to bring Suzy, but she insisted on driving her own van, which seemed prudent and appropriate to me. Wolf groused a little that we had room for both women, but I think he was hoping not having a ride home would persuade them more easily to stay.

We all ended up sitting in Wolf's kitchen. "I usually put something together myself on Sunday nights," he said, looking in the refrigerator speculatively. "Sylvia needs some time off."

"How is she?" I asked.

A Ton of Trouble

"Her shrink decided not to hospitalize her. So I guess that's good."

"What happened?" Thelma asked.

"She cut herself again," I explained. "Do you think she would like to have dinner with us?"

"You could ask her, Jo. Her room is at the end of the hall to the left. I know she misses Thelma, too," Wolf said. If I hadn't known him better I might have thought he was acting shy around Thelma.

I went down the hallway. The door was open to the room just before the end of the hall and I saw Arthur Terhune in a small office, making notes on a computer.

"I was just going to ask Sylvia if she would like to have dinner with us, how about you?"

"I've already eaten, but go ahead."

"Next time, maybe?"

He managed a wintry smile, "Certainly, next time."

I knocked and Sylvia came to the door. I was reminded again of just how tall and thin she was. "I apologize for the way I acted the other day," she whispered.

"It's okay. Would you like to have dinner with us? Thelma is there with her friend Suzy. They were cooking something when I left the kitchen, and Wolf was getting in the way."

"Thank you, but no." She withdrew back into the room. Walking past Arthur Terhune again, he looked at me. I shrugged and shook my head. He sighed and turned back to his keyboard.

When I got back to the kitchen Suzy was grilling some sausages for sandwiches and Thelma was making a salad. Wolf looked up from opening some nonalcoholic grape juice.

"She said no thanks," I said.

"Oh, well, it was a long shot." Wolf put out wine glasses and offered to get us some wine. "I don't keep it in the kitchen anymore, just so as not to tempt fate. But there's no reason my guests shouldn't indulge."

We all immediately assured him that grape juice was fine, and I could almost feel Thelma sigh in relief that Wolf was not being tempted.

"I just wondered if you went back on the Antabuse," I asked tentatively.

"Not yet. My doctor said it's not a good idea just now. But maybe I will. I'm exploring the idea with my therapist. But let's not talk about me. What happened with your project, Thelma—could you salvage any of the shoot?"

"No, it was pretty much over when the cops showed up," Thelma said. "The Manx brothers vanished, so they're out of the picture."

Wolf snorted. "Not a great loss, Thelma. I can find you five or six replacement guys with ten minutes of phone calls."

"Suzy and I may start with an adult web site while we're building back up to the videos."

"My brother can put the site up for us for free," Suzy said. "He's a computer genius."

"I'll need to see some ID that he's over eighteen." Thelma smiled, "I've seen your brother and I don't want to get into trouble corrupting minors."

Suzy laughed. "Then we'd better wait till next month. He turns eighteen in November."

There was a, "Hey, gang! Let's put on a show in the barn!" quality to their enthusiasm. But once they got down to the explicit details of what would be on the site and the web cam, I realized it was time for me to go.

On the drive back to San Francisco I realized that al-

A Ton of Trouble

though Wolf, Thelma, and Suzy fascinated me, the actual pornography they filmed made me nervous. The video I had gotten at Newburn's was still sitting unwatched on top of the television at the Pine Street condo. When I got back, I glanced at it and left it sitting there, its virginal shrink-wrap inviolate.

I sat down to make some phone calls. Harvey and Wally had called to report progress and said they would tell me in person the next morning: I called Mulligan and he greeted the news of the discovery of Monty's body with a long silence.

"You're not angry with me?" I didn't know him well enough to know what that silence meant.

"No reason to get angry, Jo. It's not like you had any part in this guy's death. But if he was involved in drug dealing, you need some backup here. Talk to Wally and Harvey about this stuff."

"They're coming over in the morning to talk about Raylene Shotwell."

"Well, get them in the loop about these drug dealers. That's the kind of thing they eat for breakfast."

"I'll keep that in mind. Last time they brought donuts."

"Then it's your turn. They like cinnamon buns, apple fritters, things like that."

The next morning I got up early enough to go to a nearby bakery—which involved trudging down one of those vertical hills and back up again. Harvey and Wally showed up at 9:00 and inhaled the cinnamon buns. The box was empty by 9:10, then they sipped coffee while debating the merits of all the bakeries in the downtown area. I would have pegged them as connoisseurs, if I hadn't seen the downscale doughnut box they had brought over last time. And yet those had been very fresh donuts. It maybe that a downscale doughnut store was one of those local treasures that tourists like myself never discovered.

As if by common accord at 9:20, they both sat back and looked at me with great satisfaction, which I somehow knew had to do with the information they had unearthed rather than with the cinnamon buns.

Wally opened up a battered old briefcase, pulled out an envelope, and extracted a handful of pictures and photocopies.

"These are the pictures with Mulligan—that's for you and him—we made some prints." He pushed those aside and I picked them up, smiling at Mulligan's picture. I didn't have a picture of him before. Now I did.

"There's Ms. Shotwell at the Friend in Need office. Nice pic," Harvey said. He picked up the envelope Wally had put on the table and took out some more pictures. "Here's Raylene Shotwell's husband back in Alabama."

"Is that a mug shot?"

"You got it," Harvey said. Both men smiled a bit grimly.

"Statutory rape," Wally said.

Harvey dealt out some photocopies of court papers and newspaper clippings. "Looks like he was trying to manufacture the illegitimate babies for adoption the old-fashioned way. The unwed, underaged mother-to-be and her family used to be part of the Shotwell congregation. They were even going to let the counseling service arrange for an adoption. But when they found out who the father was, they decided to press charges instead."

"When did this happen?"

He selected a newspaper clipping from the stack and tapped it. "Last month."

"Does Raylene know?"

"That is not clear yet." Harvey said. He looked at me candidly. "My guess is that even mentioning it here in the Bay Area will slow down the donations. They won't exactly blame the wife for the husband's being a jerk, but it won't escape their notice that she's here instead of back there—not that they want her to bring him out."

"Wow . . ." I was speechless.

"There is more." Wally handed me a sheet of paper. "We got a rundown on some of the affiliates of your Friend in Need clinics. A couple of them are doctors, but this one is a lawyer who specializes in adoption law. We talked to some people who adopted babies using his law firm. They paid a pretty high price, and some of it might have gone into the Friend in Need coffers. We need more time to check that out. But it does seem like a coincidence that the address where the lady is staying in the Bay Area is the same as the lawyer's home address."

"You mean, this last one in Jenner Ranch?" The address sounded familiar.

"You may not know to ask"—Harvey leaned back in his chair—"but that is a very fancy development on the coast in Sonoma. You don't buy a house there for less than two million."

"Interesting."

"One other thing." Wally showed me the empty envelope. "No documentation on this one, but it's a rumor on the street that the Friend in Need Centers are for white girls only."

"WHAT? Isn't that illegal?"

"Didn't say they do anything illegal. It's a private foundation. Don't know if they get any federal or state funding that would make it illegal. But they offer a lot of financial and moral support to unwed mothers—if they happen to be white. The money comes from adoptive parents looking to find a white baby. Their lawyer helps arrange adoption. The rumor in the neighborhood is that if a young woman of color walks in there in the same condition, they give her a list of other charities that can help her, and not so much as a Muni bus token."

"Wow. Has anyone ever made a formal complaint?"

Wally shrugged. "The sisters here talk to their mamas and their aunts and they know that ain't right, but it's a private charity, not a public agency—a young woman who just finds out she's pregnant has got to keep her mind on finding someone who will help her. Everyone I talked to said it wasn't fair—but what else is new?"

Wally looked at the tabletop and pushed the empty envelope back and forth a few times, then he looked at me, "Sorry. Got to push the envelope from time to time."

Harvey rolled his eyes. "If you had any idea how often I've heard that one . . ."

"Come on, Harvey, only when we get around envelopes—how often is that?"

Harvey snorted.

Wally cleared his throat. "Thing is, Jo, if your employer decided to give money to this person, I just want you to know that we're going to have to talk to some reporters we know about this place. Maybe what they're doing is legal, but people should know."

"Fine by me. I'll just tell my employer that the press is nosing around the place and why."

Both men sighed simultaneously. I realized they hadn't

been sure how I would react to that idea. "Okay." Wally said, "But Mulligan said you were getting bored with simple rifle attacks and you ran into something worse."

"I guess I did. I don't know if it's related." I told them about Monty, the possibility that he might have been involved somehow in something illegal with Steve, up to and including drug dealing."

"We'll ask around."

I told them everything I knew about Steve Farquar, which wasn't much.

After the bad news bears left I looked over the documentation. One item caught my eye. The attorney who won a religious discrimination lawsuit against the Shotwells was Sedona Yamada.

33

I had agreed to drive Wolf to his twelve-step meeting the next day, but I had to be in Baronsville to help coordinate a lineup of supersized women to stand beside Thelma at the Baronsville County Jail.

I was rather proud of myself for helping to get some other women around Thelma's size.

"It won't be easy," Sedona had said, "but the Baronsville police agreed it's the only fair way."

"It might not be that hard," I had told her. And indeed it wasn't.

Thelma and Suzy, who was an Internet fiend, helped spread an emergency call to online chat rooms and Internet mailing lists that we were looking for women around Thelma's size who lived locally and who might be available to help.

In the end there were a dozen women in Thelma's dress size who said they would be happy to take the time—two of them even offered to fly up from Southern California, but that wasn't necessary. We met at a plus-sized clothing store in Santa Rosa whose owner offered to furnish six identical outfits for the women who would be in the lineup. It was a little amazing seeing all those large women in the same room at the same time. Thelma wiped away a tear and hugged everyone.

In the end, the outfit they all wore was a simple white gauze cotton blouse and pants, with white scarves over their heads to hide their hair.

I didn't see the lineup, but Sedona told me that the look on the Baronsville police officers' faces was worth photographing when five supersized women walked in, all dressed in white pants and shirts and wearing bandannas.

After the line up we had planned to car pool to a local pizza place for a celebratory pizza. But while I sat on a park bench waiting for the women to come back out of the sheriff's office across the lawn from the old-fashioned courthouse square, I saw Elmira Jones leaving the Baronsville Police Station, looking even smaller and frailer in a pale blue dress and orthopedic sandals with support hose. She still wore the dark sunglasses and clung to the arm of a man in his sixties, just slightly taller than she was. I assumed that must have been her son, the orthodontist. I wanted to say hello, but before I could reach her, another elderly lady all in black, walking slowly with a young woman also in black, stopped her.

It was the elder Mrs. Baron, holding her granddaughter's arm and trailed by Jerry Park. The two old women stopped and greeted each other politely. "Elmira, dear, how is your eyesight holding up, what with the glaucoma and all?" Mrs. Baron asked, leaning over the shorter woman.

Elmira clutched her son's arm and leaned up into the other woman's face, "Just fine, Rose, dear. My doctor says I can still drive, and I passed the vision test for my license, but my son insists on driving me." She patted her son's arm.

"Well, don't risk your eyesight by straining yourself into blindness. Be sensible," Mrs. Baron said. Her granddaughter stayed immobile in her grip throughout the whole conversation.

"Come on, Mom," Elmira's son said.

A Ton of Trouble

The two women muttered barely audible good-byes and were walked off in opposite directions by their escorting relatives.

"Geriatric catfight?" asked a voice at my side, and I looked over to see Sedona Yamada.

"Hard to tell. How did the lineup go?"

"Perfectly. Mrs. Jones wasn't at all sure which, if any, of these women she saw near the body the night of the murder. She certainly couldn't pick Thelma out of the group. But the best part was all the women filing in. The policewoman behind the desk told her fellow officer to put his eyes back in his head." Sedona said with a chuckle.

"I've got a question."

"Sure, what is it?"

I showed her the clipping from Alabama. "You were the lawyer in this case?"

She examined it for a moment. "That's right. That was one of my famous victories."

"So you were responsible for the Shotwells' losing a great deal of money."

"No. The Shotwells were responsible for their misdeeds. I just helped some people get compensation for being wronged."

"So why is Raylene shooting at me and not you?"

"Raylene is shooting at you? Did you see her?"

"No. Maybe it was someone else. Never mind."

The six women from the lineup were coming out of the courthouse and we went to meet them, take them to lunch, then back to their respective cars.

I decided to stay in Baronsville for the evening's twelve-step meeting that I'd promised to attend with Wolf. There was no sign of Raylene Shotwell. I had no proof that she was the one who had fired at me, but it seemed like she was keeping a low profile.

Sedona and Thelma had legal matters to talk about, so I wandered down Baronsville's Main Street. The town was an odd mix of antique stores, trendy cafés, and ruthlessly practical convenience stores that sold the same wines as the quaint restaurants, but also sold a variety of items aimed at truckers, travelers, and farmers. Once I left the immediate vicinity of the police station, the pace slowed a bit, and it became clear that Monday was not a major traffic day. There were some October tourists, but most of the touring world was at work, saving up for the weekend.

Wolf had asked me to pick him up at 6:00. I wasn't too hungry after the late lunch, so an hour beforehand I stopped for a cup of coffee and a piece of pie to fortify me for an evening of diet talk. I'd been to these meetings in my early teens, when my aunt who raised me was desperate to find something to change my shape into something she thought more suitable. Like every other diet, the ones this group offered had caused some weight loss, followed by a regain of more than the original loss. What depressed me about the group was that they seemed to be pleased to repeat that pattern over and over and to blame themselves endlessly when it failed to work. I did not look forward to keeping my mouth shut and listening to this. If Angela Baron didn't show, I vowed to sneak over into Wolf's meeting and trade the battle of the bulge for the battle with the bottle.

I pulled into the parking lot at Wolf's a little before 6:00 and rang the bell. A few minutes later he came out, but as he was getting into the car, Sylvia came out the door, too. Wolf appeared to be as surprised as I was to see her.

"Can I go, too?" She asked.

"Of course," Wolf said, opening the door for her.

"Don't tell my father, okay?"

"Don't worry." Wolf closed the door and got into the back-seat behind her, patting her shoulder. "It really is anonymous. We won't tell anyone."

We were startled enough that none of us spoke much the first minute or two. Then Sylvia asked, "What kind of meetings are there tonight?"

Wolf counted on his fingers, "There's an Alcoholics Anonymous meeting that I'm going to. Jo is going to the Overeaters Anonymous meeting."

Sylvia looked over at me from the passenger seat. I nodded. I was not looking forward to this, and I figured the less I said the better at this point.

"Is that all tonight?"

"I think there was an Al-Anon meeting earlier in the day for families. Tomorrow there's an NA meeting."

"And the *N* is for . . . ?"

"Narcotics."

"I want to go to that one."

"I'll make sure you get a ride," Wolf said. A few minutes later we arrived at the community center. The Lutheran Church next door was darkened, but a steady stream of people were entering the community center. Wolf went to the room to the left with the AA sign and I took a deep breath and went into the OA room. There were only three women there—all about my size.

Two of the three were setting up a circle of several chairs and a table with literature, coffee, and a donation box, while the third woman sat looking as if she wanted to be anywhere but there. That made two of us.

The woman setting up the last chair greeted me cheerfully. "You're new. Welcome to our meeting. There may be a few more people coming."

There was no sign of Angela Baron.

Another woman, who was probably about half my weight, walked in. I could see from the look on her face that she was facing her worst nightmare. At the same time there was an air of puzzlement. How could these fat women help her not to become like them? Before anyone could say anything, she turned and fled the room.

The woman who was setting up the coffee started the meeting. "I know there aren't very many of us here, but somehow just being here with you makes me feel better."

I took a deep breath, tried to concentrate on what everyone was saying.

"Is it your first time here?" The coffee lady asked.

"I went to one of these in Seattle," I said. "I met a woman named Angela who told me there was a meeting here."

"Oh, Angela, I know her," the chair lady said. The coffee lady gave her a nasty look. Maybe it wasn't acceptable to say anything about someone else. I made a note to talk to her later, if I could extract her from the coffee lady's grip.

The next hour passed very slowly. The coffee lady had a lot to say. We went round the circle, which I hadn't exactly anticipated, so I simply said I was new and here to learn. They gave me some information. Each of the three followed different food plans, which sounded like diets to me. We read some inspirational literature and somewhere in the universe, in answer to my silent prayer, some higher power decreed that the meeting could end early.

The coffee lady closed up shop and went to take the coffeepot into the kitchen. I helped the chair lady fold up and stow the chairs away and asked if it had been a long time since she saw Angela there.

"Angela doesn't come here anymore. I think she was frustrated because she always gained back more than she lost." We folded and stacked the last chair and went out into the front room of the community center. "Besides," she leaned close to whisper, "there was this guy who goes to the AA meetings. I think he was some kind of celebrity or something, but I never heard of him. Anyway, he's notorious for flirting with the OA girls. He never bothered me, but I saw him talking to Angela, and Angie is married. Very married, if you get my drift. But he really liked her a lot. You could see he lit up when she walked into the room. I think she was flattered and she liked flirting just a little. But maybe the guy who drove her to the meeting tattled on her. It wasn't her husband—he's rich and can't be bothered to drive his own wife over here. But the young guy who drove her was this big muscle-bound tank of a guy who just sat on the sofa over there and waited. Never went to any of the meetings."

Jerry Parks. "You think maybe the driver told the husband about the flirtation?"

The chair lady gasped, and I turned to see Angela Baron walking into the room. She saw me and I went over to meet her.

Both of us nodded to the chair lady, who turned and went out, perhaps embarrassed to be caught gossiping.

"Hi," Angela said, "I recognize you from the funeral. Are you Wolf Lambert's girlfriend?"

"No. But I did come here with him tonight."

She drew close and whispered, "Are you in those films? I don't recognize you."

"Uh, no. You mean, you've seen his films?" I whispered

also, trying not to glance around to see who might be listening.

"His films changed my life," Angie said. "Nothing has been the same since."

"Uh. Okay." I gathered the last of my wits around me. "I'm not Wolf's girlfriend, but he did say you might come tonight, I was hoping to meet you."

"I can't stay long, but come see me at home. Any time is fine. I have something of Wolf's that I need to return. Please come tomorrow!"

At that moment Jerry Parks walked into the room, and Angela clasped my hand briefly. "Is the OA meeting over yet?"

"They ended early."

She smiled. "They do that sometimes if not too many people come."

"There were four of us."

She patted my elbow. "See you later."

The AA meeting was still going strong when she conferred with Jerry a few minutes later and left. Finally Wolf and Sylvia and another seven or eight people came out of the AA meeting, talking quietly. I was glad to see that Sylvia seemed a little heartened by the meeting. She was talking to another woman who patted her hand when it was time to go. Wolf was clearly starved for human interaction and very disappointed that the OA meeting had already broken up and everyone was gone. I managed to get him to go after half an hour of coffee and conversation by pointing out that I still had over an hour's drive back to San Francisco.

34

When I got back to the city, though, I found myself un-expectedly restless. The video sitting unopened on the television set drew my attention and I decided to bite the bullet and watch it. I did not look forward to what I was about to do. It was ironic that so many people eagerly anticipated watching these videos and I was dreading it. I went down to the liquor store on the corner and fortified myself with a bottle of peach brandy—hearkening back to my college bad girl drinking days—locked the door, closed the curtains, and turned on the VCR.

Big, Bad Biker Babes was worse than I might have imagined. Even before the opening credits there were several minutes of previews of other films and sex-talk phone numbers. I started out fast-forwarding through that.

The film began with some wooden dialogue. I wasn't sure if the humor in the dialogue was intentional. The obligatory thirty seconds of plot started with an improbably scrawny-looking biker asking a very big brunette who wore ankle-strap six-inch heels and denim cutoffs and a leather jacket, "Wanna see my hog?" It did make sense that the action would then move to a bed, improbably located in a garage with a Harley-Davidson as a headboard. It was literally a dirty movie.

There was no sign of Thelma. Something about the biker and girlfriend interlude began to make me very nervous. He never took off his motorcycle boots for one thing, which made him look silly. The woman also kept on her spike heels. I wondered if that was because the garage floor was dirty.

The woman had a glazed look, as if she were drugged or embarrassed. She might have been enjoying herself tremendously but she wasn't paying any attention to her partner. He was shoving her around on the mattress as if she were an anatomically correct inanimate object and keeping his eyes fixed on the wall. The disconnection made the whole thing look disastrously professional rather than personal. Livestock would have made a more personal connection.

I couldn't stand much of that without hitting the fast-forward button. It went on forever and suddenly I remembered why I had walked out on the last X-rated movie I'd seen. It had included a sort of rape fantasy that left me ice-cold. In this film, the man had also been pushing the woman around. He wasn't being rough, just pushing her down onto the bed in a way that reminded me of an evening in college. I might have called it a date rape if I'd ever heard of such a thing. One of those occasions when saying no has utterly no effect on the proceedings whatsoever.

Rather than arousing me, this film reminded me of the kind of unlubricious sex that makes premature ejaculation a consummation devoutly to be wished for. I shut the video off for a moment, recalling that night with a sick feeling. How it seemed as if it would never end. I had escaped from the man as soon as he disengaged. He called the next day; I told him not to call again. He was puzzled at being rejected. I wasted a few minutes trying to explain. "I told you no, and you went ahead, anyway."

A Ton of Trouble

"If you didn't want to do it, why didn't you just slap me?" I hung up on him, but in retrospect I realized I had never slapped anyone in my life. The thought that if I had hit him he might have returned the favor didn't help much.

At least I could fast-forward the film. If only I could have done the same with that awful date. I fast-forwarded as nature took its course on-screen. The famous money shot occurred— semen was produced, spread all over every available surface and applauded by all participants. Fast-forwarding cut way down on the queasy feeling that this produced, even though the thought of it being piña colada mix added some charm. So far, fast-forwarding was the best part of the film.

I was relieved to see that the next interlude featured Thelma and she was not wearing shoes. Indeed, the scene had moved out to a blanket in the backyard. She could never have walked across the grass in shoes. Thelma was sitting on the blanket and one of the Manx brothers appeared to help her spread oil all over her generous proportions. I could see why she had caught Wolf's eye. Unlike the other lady, who had vanished into her own inner world, Thelma flirted and giggled and made eye contact with Rod Manx.

As soon as they got down to business, Ringo Manx appeared, lurking in the background, wearing sunglasses, rings, and black leather pants. Thelma welcomed him as well.

Rod Manx kept his sandals on and Ringo also kept the dark sunglasses on. Either he was afraid someone would make off with his sunglasses, or he was making a fashion statement.

The dialogue didn't have a lot to recommend it. It mostly consisted of, "Yeah. Yeah. Oh, yeah." With the occasional "Ooooh." But I had to admit that considering what they were doing, hardly anyone would pay attention to what they were saying. The three of them proceeded to go at it like minks.

Or, rather as minks are reputed to do. Mercifully, if there was a film that showed minks going at it, I had been spared that footage.

The last scene showed Thelma and Suzy and played up Thelma's pale skin and coppery hair against the chocolate tones of Suzy's skin and hair. That was tender and affectionate, and contained helpful tips on inspired use of vibrators.

As the film rewound I felt anxious and irritated rather than aroused. I guessed Wolf's films would be better. Who knows? Maybe Thelma would make the kind of film that would turn what I had just seen into a work of art. Or most likely I was missing the point of the whole thing.

I was restless, so I got out the material Wally and Harvey had brought and looked it over again. I put it in its envelope and sat for a long time staring at the wall, not seeing anything I liked very much. I even pushed the envelope across the table and managed a smile at the bad news bears' joke. Then I took out the list of supporters of the Friend in Need project, opened up my laptop, and logged onto the Internet. By midnight I had a list, which I e-mailed to Ambrose for some comments. Then I looked for web sites. These people were definitely the pillars of the community. But one of them, Harvey Archambault, had some interesting links. I didn't trust what I was seeing, so I decided to ask Ambrose to look into it personally.

35

The next morning was Thursday. I had decided to see Angela Baron in the afternoon, but I called Ambrose first. I explained that I was going up to Jenner Ranch to pay a call on Raylene Shotwell, or at least her hosts, the Archambaults.

"Yes, I got your e-mail. Did you know Mrs. Archambault is a social acquaintance of Mrs. Madrone?"

"No. I didn't. But that is interesting."

"Are you going to call first? She may not be there."

"In a way it doesn't matter."

The house I was going to visit was north of San Francisco and up a winding road through redwoods to the ocean. The wind off the ocean was intense, and the landscape had a scraped-clean kind of beauty under the hard blue sky.

I remember reading that owners of homes here had to meet certain architectural restrictions that included blending into the landscape with minimal visual jarring. The landscape itself was assertive. I parked in a turnaround at the end of the driveway. The parking area on the bluff that held the huge house faced a wind-torn vista of the Pacific Ocean, as did the Archambault home. By the time I got out and locked the car, the windshield was already beginning to scum up with sea salt.

Raylene Shotwell's car was not parked in front of the house, but it looked as if the house was rooted deeply on the hill. I was betting on a sunken garage.

Nanette Archambault met me at the door. I was impressed. From the looks of the house, I had expected a maid to answer. For a moment I was startled. She was in her mid-sixties, and holding the illusion of at least a decade younger with tastefully marinated auburn hair and deft plastic surgery. She was dressed in organic cotton with a linen jacket for a casual day out—no doubt spending money in places with noble causes behind them.

"I was just leaving," she stood in the doorway, blocking it.

I held out the envelope I had prepared. "This is for your houseguest." I had written "Raylene Shotwell—Personal and Confidential" on the envelope.

"Come in for a moment," she turned on her heel and led the way through an exquisite foyer with a skylight and deep Persian carpeting. She opened a door and I followed her into another room that managed to be light and airy, thanks to the huge windows looking out on the ocean and despite the blustery weather outside and the fact that the walls were crammed with hunting trophies and a locked glass case displaying guns from antique to state of the art.

Neither of us made a comment about the decor. She did not invite me to sit down and we both stood by a massive stone fireplace while she tore open the envelope without regard for the addressee. I noted that in accepting her hospitality, one forfeited privacy.

A Ton of Trouble

The envelope contained the article about the statutory rape case and another brief paragraph suggesting that Raylene and her husband were accused of, on some occasions, collecting money from two or three couples for the same baby.

"You shouldn't have put your dogs on Raylene," Nanette said with the same Teflon tone that she had used to invite me in. "She's an unstable woman. When she heard someone was investigating her husband—he's really her Achilles' heel in so many ways—well, she flew straight back to Alabama. I'll tell her you stopped by." She handed me back the clipping and envelope. "I wouldn't want to take the satisfaction of your little sadistic ploy away from you. Perhaps you'll want to follow her there and give her this yourself."

"Actually she was following me, and shooting at me."

"Come on, Ms. Fuller, admit that you were baiting her. She's a simple person, very energetic and very useful to us. You did ruin her dream of fighting evil here in our modern Babylon. But if she wanted you dead, you probably would be. She's an excellent shot. Maybe I should have let her take the elephant gun." Nannette gestured to the wall of weapons above the fireplace.

"So you run the Friend in Need program? You don't look like you're hurting exactly; what's the big deal about one donation?"

Nanette's eyes narrowed and she spoke through her teeth. "It's not the money, you ignorant fool." She took a step forward. We were the same height and she looked muscular. I wondered if she took a martial arts class—Society Matron Kick Boxing or something. Then there were all those invisible servants, who would no doubt come running to aid her. "The Madrone Foundation's endorsement of our work is worth far more than Alicia would ever see fit to dole out in her puny little women's grants. We want that prestige and you are not going to stand in our way."

"Mrs. Archambault, all I can say is, my opinion is my own and I don't make those decisions."

"Do you think Mrs. Madrone will approve of your moonlighting with pornographers, drug traffickers, and murderers?"

"Nice talking to you. Give my best to Raylene, if you ever talk to her again—defective instrument that she is."

I didn't realize that I was holding my breath till I made it successfully out the front door, down the walk. I looked at my car. Facing the salt wind off the ocean, my windshield was coated already. Then I exhaled and took another deep breath. Getting into the car, my hands were unaccountably shaking. I took a moment to clean the windshield and as soon as I started the engine I used the windshield wipers again. Nanette Archambault watched me from the doorway until finally I drove off. It seemed to take several minutes, but it was probably only about forty-five seconds.

I'd been scheduled to see Angela Baron, but I was not eager to go. I stopped in Glen Ellen for a sandwich. The drive through the wine country was soothing. The weekday traffic was reasonable. I was no longer shaking, but I decided not to take a chance on coffee and opted for a vitamin-fortified juice drink instead. At last, I could put it off no longer and I headed for the Baron Winery. It was up the road from Lambert's Lair, up a winding road that ended against a steep hillside. The winery itself was more than a hundred years old—a limestone building that terminated in tunnels carved out of limestone over a century earlier. Stone pillars framed the winery gates.

A Ton of Trouble

Several cars were parked in the visitor's lot, and even on a weekday afternoon, the tasting room was doing a brisk business.

The Baron family compound was separated from the winery by a stand of redwood and bay trees and yet another inner, more businesslike wrought-iron fence, like a row of spears with sharp points and metal signs at intervals announcing no trespassing and electronic surveillance. The hospitality extended to winery guests did not extend to the Baron home.

I was expected, so the uniformed security guard in a concealed stone gatehouse inside the fence examined my ID picture, comparing it to me, noted my license plate, and admitted me to the grounds of the family home. Another, shorter, driveway wound through several yards of trees and over a small bridge that spanned a canyon dividing the property yet again with moatlike efficiency. The home itself was 1890s elegant, with gingerbread and witches-cap cupolas in the Queen Anne–Victorian style. I noted that the Barons had built a more modern wing behind the Victorian facade, although it mimicked its predecessor with similar trim and lines. I parked and walked to the door.

36

T he interior of the Barons' house was even more opulent than the Archambault home. The maid who let me in was clearly expecting me. She led me to a first-floor sitting room where Angela Baron beckoned me in. She was sitting on a loveseat with gold-and-red-striped upholstery that suited her dramatic coloring. She was almost as large as Thelma, but I was getting more used to looking at supersized people, and Wolf's point about her beauty was well taken. She looked a lot younger than the late forty–something she probably was. This was clearly her private room—my guess was it adjoined her bedroom. Coffee, tea, and cookies were set out on a small, low table. I wondered how many visitors Angela had and whether her husband was ever among them. The one incongruous note in the tasteful rose-and-beige-toned room was an open lap-top computer sitting quietly in the corner with its screensaver on.

Angela Baron must have noticed my eyes straying to the computer.

"My best friend," she said with a rueful shrug. "Thank you for coming. I hope I can trust you."

I sat next to her in the chair she indicated. It really was quite close considering that I scarcely knew her. She was wearing a perfume with strong vanilla undertones.

"Wonderful perfume," I said.

"I have it custom blended from a perfume shop on Royal Street in New Orleans." She smiled and sighed. "I was there ten years ago. I used to travel more, when I was—smaller. Now, well we haven't traveled in years, but I buy it by mail— I'll send you some."

"That's very kind of you, but there's no need."

"Oh, but I'm asking you a favor. I'm going to ask you right now, in case we're interrupted. Could you please return this to Wolf Lambert?" She held out an envelope that clearly contained two videotapes. I took it and looked at it. "Please, put it in your purse now. I can't afford for Carlo to see."

I stuffed it in my purse, which was already a bit full. The bulky two tapes barely made it in.

Angela sighed, relaxing a little. "Thank you so much. I knew I could trust you. Wolf doesn't understand how it is with Carlo. Not that Wolf and I did anything wrong."

I nodded. "He told me you've never had a conversation that wasn't in front of several other people."

"That's true. And when I go out, Jerry is always with me. He's totally devoted to our family. Wishes he was part of the family in fact. He can tell Carlo that I've never been alone with anyone when I go out. I know Carlo will ask and he trusts Jerry. He should trust me, too, after nearly thirty years of marriage, but—well, there's the computer." She glanced at the offending machine as if it might say something to incriminate her.

"You mean you contacted Wolf by computer."

She nodded. "It was mostly harmless. We sent each other those Instant Message things. I never even e-mailed Wolf. I didn't want to leave a record on the computer. But I've been so alone since my daughter left home. We weren't too close, even the last few years she was at home. I started out in the chat rooms just to have someone to talk to. Wolf was there a lot. We saw each other at the twelve-step meetings. It was fun to flirt and have someone tell me I was delightful. We never talked in person with any privacy. On-line, there was a way we could meet, just to talk one-on-one. I know it was insane. I told him my husband would be murderously jealous and he said my husband had no right to monopolize my beauty if he wasn't going to appreciate it."

She began to cry. I was getting a little misty, too.

"Do you know how long it has been since anyone used the word 'beauty' in regard to me?"

"I understand," I murmured. I did. But I'm not sure she heard me. I had never been isolated the way she had and maybe I didn't truly understand, but she went on.

"I did meet him alone once. Jerry didn't know. I told Carlo I had a doctor's appointment. Jerry drove me and he usually waits in the car and reads the paper, so I met Wolf in the hospital coffee shop. We talked for two hours. You know how flirtatious he is, you met him. He offered to sweep me off my feet and take me away from all this. I tried to explain about Carlo's business, but Wolf seemed to think he had enough money and status so that Carlo would never dare touch him. I wasn't so sure. I was so worried." A tear slipped out of her eye and down her cheek.

I let her cry for a while. Just handed her tissues and patted her shoulder. Finally she said, "I know, I'm a fool. But I was so lonely. He told me he adored me. He offered to take me away from all this. It clouded my judgment and I told him we must never meet again. But I kept chatting with him on the Internet. I never kept a record of any message from him. Not

A Ton of Trouble

that Carlo ever looked at my computer, but just in case." She took a deep breath. I took a deep breath, too, terrified of what her husband might have done to her.

"Did your husband find out?" I said—realizing for the first time that we were both whispering. If her husband had the room bugged, we were toast.

"No." She stared at me wildly. "No. He never has and it must not happen. I told Wolf we could never be together the way he wanted. And, and then the videos came in the mail with a beautiful note about how we could only be together in fantasy."

"Wolf sent you these videos?"

"Yes. I know it's strange. I never gave him my address, but of course, he knew who I was and where I lived, because he's just next door. I had to burn the note. Thank God Carlo didn't see it. Or these."

I blinked in surprise. "And you just want me to take the videos back."

"Please."

There was a brief, curt knock and Carlo Baron walked quickly into the room followed by Jerry Park. His lip was curled in a sneer and I felt fear wash over me as if a bucket of ice water had been dumped down my spine.

"I always like to meet my wife's friends," he walked past Angela as if she weren't there and stood over me, looking me over. "I like a woman with a little meat on her bones."

I stared at him in silence. If this was flattery, he needed lessons.

"A little meat, you understand, not a whole butcher shop." He looked at Jerry Parks, who simply looked uncomfortable.

"Gee, I would have thought you were older than fourteen, but it seems like you're socially stuck around junior high school level when it comes to talking to girls, huh?"

"You didn't understand me?"

"Oh, I understand you all right. You're socially retarded."
I stood up to leave.

"Wait a minute," he nodded to Jerry, who blocked my way.
"I saw you on the security camera. You didn't have that bulge
in your purse when you came in. What's in there? Open it up,
Jerry."

Jerry took my purse and opened it up. The envelope with
the two videos popped up from the top where I had crammed
them in. Jerry handed it to Carlo, who opened the envelope
without hesitation. I guess this was Open Other People's Mail
Day.

Carlo looked at the videos. The covers left nothing to the
imagination. He turned to glare at his wife. "Angela, you want
to explain this?"

She held up her head and grasped the arms of the chair,
levering herself to her feet.

"Come with me, Carlo, and I'll explain. In private." She
walked with great dignity toward the side door.

Carlo Baron gestured at me and pointed to a sliding door
that led to a small patio, "You. Wait out there. I got to talk
to my wife."

Jerry opened the door to the patio and gestured for me to
go out first.

We stood awkwardly. A moment later the awkwardness
was compounded when both of us realized that a trick of the
building's vents brought the couple's voices through the open
door to us.

"Angela, you watch these films? This is the trash that
bastard Wolf Lambert makes. Jerry said you talk to him at the
OA meetings, what does this mean?"

A Ton of Trouble

"Jerry has been with me every second I spoke to him, and I never touched the man. Not even a handshake. We only talked. He was nice. You haven't been nice for a long time."

"You talked. It was nice. Did you look at those films? Is that what you talked about?"

"Maybe we could learn something from those films."

"From trash like that? I don't see how."

"Maybe I could show you how." The rest of what she said was lost, as if she had lowered her voice.

There were a couple of murmured comments, then Carlo's said gruffly, "You would do that? You're mother of a grown child, for God's sake."

"I'm still a woman, Carlo. You seem to have forgotten that." I looked at Jerry out of the corner of my eye. He was blushing. "I can still do this. Or this," Angela's voice was husky.

"Oh, my God." There was a very clear squeak of bedsprings.

Jerry and I both stared out at the decorative fountain while the noises that filtered through the terrace door left little to the imagination, although the words didn't make a lot of sense. Lots of incoherent gasping and moaning.

The sounds died down after a while, or possibly they had moved to another part of the room. They appeared to have totally forgotten Jerry and me. I glanced over and saw that Jerry was looking at me with a speculative glance. I shook my head firmly, but tried to look sympathetic. Neither of us said anything. After several minutes, I got tired of standing and sat on the little wrought-iron bench next to the fountain. Half an hour passed.

Then I heard a muttering from the outside of the tall wooden fence that shielded the patio. A gate I hadn't noticed before opened and a small, spare, white-haired woman came into view, wearing khaki pants and blouse, with a grubby garden smock, its pockets bulging. At first I didn't recognize her, but when she met my eyes with an eaglelike gaze, from the bend in her spine, the white hair, and the chain that held her glasses on—these must be her gardening glasses because the jet beads were replaced with silver—it was Carlo Baron's mother.

"Jerry," she said, as if heeling a dog.

"Mrs. Baron," he said reverently.

"Where is my son?"

"Uh, he's with Mrs. Baron," Jerry said, leaving it at that.

"Is she okay?"

"I think so." I could actually hear Jerry gulp.

"Well?" She made a dismissive gesture. "Don't keep me waiting. Get him."

"Uh, I got orders. I'm watching that—uh, lady." He tilted his head at me.

At that moment all three of us were startled to hear screaming coming from inside the room. For a moment I thought of intervening, but the tone of the screaming made me pause. Mrs. Baron was listening thoughtfully. She met my eyes. "That's married people's stuff," she said unexpectedly, reaching up and pinching me on the cheek.

"*Ouch!*"

"If you ever get married, you'll understand." Mrs. Baron stuck her head in the patio door and yelled, "CARLO!" so loudly that Jerry and I both jumped.

"If you can hear them, they can hear you, huh?" she said with an eloquent nod.

She went back into the sitting room and stood staring at the door Carlo and Angela had retreated through. A moment

later, Carlo came through it, hastily tucking in his shirt and
buttoning his trousers and, despite his gray hair, looking like
a schoolchild caught playing hooky. Angela came right behind
him, shyly adjusting her dress.

"I'm happy to see you two acting more like a normal couple. But you should know that when you're standing on the
patio, you can hear everything that happens in there." She
gestured to the bedroom.

The two lowered their heads like chastised teenagers. "It's
your own business if you want everyone to know what you're
doing. But if you wanted to be sensible, let Jerry escort this—
lady out of here and go to the master bedroom, where you both
should be sleeping, anyway. The whole world can't hear what
you do."

"That's okay mama, we—"

"I never approved of this separate bedroom arrangement.

"Mama—"

"Did you hear what I said?"

"Yes, mama."

Carlo glanced at Jerry briefly.

I didn't wait for Jerry to get the idea. "Happy to leave." I
turned to go, and Jerry was hot on my heels.

I exited the front door, escorted by the silent Jerry.

37

Raylene Shotwell's Cadillac was parked outside the gates of the Baron Winery. She was standing next to the car, leaning against the driver's-side door, looking out at the fields of grapes. I didn't see any weapons in her hands. On impulse, I stopped and got out of the car.

"I was just curious what you were doing in San Francisco away from your own family. Do you really believe that God has one plan for women and another one for men?"

"That's exactly right. As a woman I should be listening, when God and my husband talk, not always telling them what to do. Maybe if you listened you'd have a man who would marry you, instead of running around with baby killers and prostitutes and pornographers."

"Why aren't you home then, listening to your husband?"

"Because God has different plans for me. I'm here to point people in God's direction."

"Your version of God—and coincidentally one that profits you financially. That's really what your husband agrees with, isn't it? As long as the money keeps pouring in and you never ask him to do any of the stuff you're pushing on other people."

"You told Nanette Archambault, didn't you?"

"Told her what?"

A Ton of Trouble

"About my husband, being persecuted."

"You mean prosecuted." I couldn't resist correcting her.

"I know what I mean." Her voice was tight and I could see her control was very close to snapping. I didn't see a gun anywhere near her hands. The rifle was probably in the car.

I admitted to myself that this woman brought out my worst side, and clearly it was mutual. I sighed. "I didn't have to tell Nanette about the—uh, your husband's latest legal problems, Raylene. I found out about it, but she already knew."

Raylene Shotwell was speechless for a moment. "That is a lie!"

"No, it's true."

Her straight posture collapsed and Raylene bent over. For a moment I thought she might faint "I really thought it was over. He swore he would stop."

It was sadistic, but I couldn't stop myself from saying, "Maybe if you were at home, doing the wifely duty thing . . ." Even as I said it, I realized it was my way of getting back at her for saying no man would ever have me, but I knew I would pay for that remark.

She looked at me with pure, distilled hatred in her eyes, "He's always strayed. He's weak. But he doesn't mean to be evil. You do. I will destroy that evil—no matter what form it takes. And I will destroy you."

She got into the car a little unsteadily and started the engine. I was vastly relieved that she hadn't whipped out a firearm of some sort and killed me on the spot.

I watched her drive away, reflecting that I should have come up with words aimed at defusing the situation. Instead I appeared to have relit the fuse. My fondest hope was that Mr. Eugene Shotwell would receive the first target strike. But I wasn't so sure about that.

38

I looked over my shoulder and in my rearview mirror a lot on the drive back to San Francisco. I also cursed my own stupidity at inciting Raylene. I called Wally and Harvey even before I called Mulligan when I got back to the Pine Street condo. Mulligan suggested I come home and reasonably mentioned that Harvey and Wally were out chasing down leads on what kind of drug dealers Steve Farquar might have been involved with.

"There's no one there to protect you twenty-four hours a day, Jo. Why don't you stay in the condo there—it's a security building, right?"

"I guess so. Everything's locked and there's a guard at the front desk."

"Minimal, but better than nothing. Finish your report and come on home where I can keep an eye on you 24-7."

"Yes, sir." Ironic that my encounter with Raylene was encouraging me to be obedient to the man in my life because I was suddenly afraid I might not survive to see him again. It wasn't right, but I decided my goal would be to live to fight another day.

I sighed and got out my laptop computer and began to

type up a report. I put in the rumors of prejudice and the fact that local newspapers were investigating along with the women's experiences just exactly as they had told me. I realized that this was one of those situations where Mrs. Madrone's personal views would probably make the decision. My job was to give her my opinion.

I managed to finish the report before it was fully dark. I printed out the last page and put on a coat to go in search of dinner. Maybe the place with the key lime pie.

A knock at the door startled me. I went and cautiously looked through the peephole and saw Jerry Parks filling the viewer. Standing next to him, was a man in a dark suit, displaying a badge and laminated photo ID that read Federal Bureau of Investigation. Another two men, in dark suits, were standing there. I called down to the front desk and the guard there said they had checked the man's ID.

I opened the door and they crowded in. "Excuse us, ma'am," the man who had been displaying his ID said and turned to Jerry, "This is her?" Jerry nodded miserably.

"You're not with the FBI, are you?" I reached for the cell phone I had put on the table, got it, and managed to hit the speed-dial 911.

"You and your security guard should know that those badges are a dime a dozen, and so are good photo IDs." The man shoved his ID into his breast pocket and took the phone out of my hands before the 911 operator could answer.

"What are you doing here?" I asked Jerry.

"We brought him along to get in the door. You did seem to be cozy last time we saw you," said the man who had shown me the badge. He seemed immensely pleased with his own cleverness.

Another man came into the apartment through the still
open door. He closed it behind him. The phone rang a moment
later.

The man with the badge threw it against the back wall. It
stopped ringing. He grabbed me by the arm. I noticed now
that his friend had a gun casually pressed against Jerry's side.

"Come along with us and we won't have to cuff you."

"You can't be from the FBI." I was confused but certain
of that one fact.

"Let's put it this way. The security guard downstairs thinks
we're from the FBI, so if we handcuffed you and dragged you
downstairs by brute force, he would just think we were doing
our job. So come along and come quietly."

I followed them quietly, but as we passed the security
guard I yelled, "This is a kidnapping! Call Ambrose Terrell.
Get these guys' license plate."

"Come on, crazy lady." The man holding my arm twisted
it so painfully that I cried out and looked over to the security
guard, "Drugs," he said, "It makes 'em wild."

We got as far as the building front door when I heard
gunfire and the thick glass of the front door shattered under
the man's hand. Everyone instinctively jumped back. I hesitated an instant and I looked at Jerry.

He wasn't as slow as advertised. The man with the gun
pressed into Jerry's side screamed as Jerry broke his wrist. I
threw my full weight against the man holding me and stamped
as hard as I could on his foot. He staggered sideways and let
go of me for an instant. I broke away. The man with the badge
and his friends were taking cover around the sides of the door
and getting out their guns. Another rifle shot. I stepped
through the door, walking carefully through the broken glass
on the sidewalk. People were running, and I simply walked.

The rifle fire followed me, but the men in the building were now returning fire. I walked through the mess of glass and dodged running tourists, then turned into the underground parking garage.

"I've got my keys. They made me drive," a voice said way too close to me. I looked back and saw Jerry.

"Where's your car? They're not going to stay in there long."

We could have gone straight to the nearest police station, but I didn't have a clue where that was, and the security guard accepting those FBI badges made me nervous. Jerry opened the car door with the remote on his key chain. We both piled into the black Mercedes and exited the parking garage a few moments ahead of a fleet of San Francisco Police Department units that blocked off Pine Street just behind us. I didn't hear any more gunfire. Had someone stopped shooting, or had the shooter been stopped?

Jerry drove at normal speed up Pine Street, turned right on Van Ness and then left on Lombard, heading for the Golden Gate Bridge.

"Did they kidnap you in Baronsville?" I asked.

"Yeah. Outside the winery gates."

"Do you know if they hurt the Barons?"

He glanced at me as if I had slapped him. "I don't know. I hope not."

The ninety-minute drive was tense. The beautiful landscape along 101 and then Highway 12 went past unremarked in the growing darkness. Neither of us spoke. Jerry drove straight to the Baron Winery and used a remote to open the gate.

"What if those guys are there, or their people are there? Shouldn't we call the police first?"

Jerry looked at me. "I don't know, but Mr. Baron will know."

"But, Jerry, they might have him tied up or something."

"I'm not going to call the police until Mr. Baron says so."

I looked around the Mercedes for a car phone, a weapon, anything. But there was only the remote garage door opener, and we drove into the Baron's garage. I followed Jerry into the house. He went straight to a suitably baronial room with plush red Turkish carpets, leather armchairs, a fireplace, and walls of bookshelves interspersed with pictures of the estate in bygone days. This must be Carlo Baron's office. It was deserted.

I followed him through the house. He ran into a maid, a subdued Filipino woman in her forties, and told her it was urgent he speak to Mr. Baron. She said, "Last I saw, Mr. Baron went into Mrs. Baron's room." Then she shyly looked away.

I followed Jerry to the back of the house, where big Angie's suite opened out onto the first-floor patio. He knocked at the door, "Excuse me, Mr. Baron, there's a problem."

There was a muffled answer. I looked at Jerry, but he refused to meet my eyes. A full minute went past and then Carlo Baron appeared, buttoning his shirtfront. He saw me, then cast a look over his shoulder and opened the door. "Come in, what is it?"

"I was taken at gunpoint outside the winery gates by some guys with FBI badges and ID cards."

Baron looked at him quizzically and then looked at me. He reached out and with an oddly intimate gesture picked a piece of thick glass off the collar of my blouse.

"That must have come from the Pine Street glass doors when they shattered," I said. I hadn't known it was there.

"What's she doing here?" Baron said to Jerry.

"They forced me to drive to Pine Street. They knew the

address and the apartment number, they told the security guard they were with the FBI. They weren't with the FBI, boss."

"Yeah," he said thoughtfully.

"They said as much when they came into my apartment. They wanted Jerry to identify me."

"Where are they?" Baron started to fasten his cuffs and glanced back at the door where his cufflinks no doubt were, along with his shoes, I realized, looking down at his bare feet. He settled for rolling up his sleeves.

"We left them under rifle fire." I said, half smiling at the irony.

"What?"

"I think it's a woman who's been stalking me because I got in the way of a charitable donation she was hoping to get."

Baron narrowed his eyes at me, uncertain whether I was joking.

"Really. She shot at Monty Johns and me when we were talking in his backyard. A couple of people have seen her with a thirty-ought-six hunting rifle. But I don't think she's the one who killed Monty down in LA."

"Monty, who used to work for me, is dead? I thought he just took a few days off." Baron looked confused.

"Someone shot him and dropped him in a swimming pool down there. I think the guys who kidnapped Jerry and were about to get me might be connected with that."

"It's because I know who killed Steve," Jerry said softly.

Baron looked at him thoughtfully.

"I was following him when he quarreled with Arthur Terhune about Arthur's daughter."

"Just a minute." Baron went to the telephone next to the computer in the corner and punched in a number from memory. "Artie, it's Carlo. Get over here. Not the winery, the residence. Come to my wife's sitting room in the back. Yes, you're right, you don't work for me, anymore. But I need to see you now, Artie—it's about Sylvia." He looked up and realized we were still standing in the doorway. "Come on inside."

Angela Baron came through the opposite door, her huge body majestically swaying in an opulent caftan and gold sandals. "Would you like some refreshments? Or maybe you'd like to freshen up." She gestured to me. "There's a bathroom through there."

Carlo watched his wife cross the room and brush past him on the way to her chair. He blushed like a teenager. I turned and walked through the bedroom to the bathroom. The bed had been clumsily remade but the blankets and sheets were slightly tangled. The room smelled of sandalwood and sex. I noted a bottle of massage oil on the bedside table and a couple of rumpled towels on the floor. The bathroom was still slightly steamy.

I used the toilet, washed my hands, and splashed cold water on my face, which was wide-eyed and sweaty. I hesitated and then combed my hair with big Angie's comb. That seemed more reasonable than my other option, which was to use my fingers.

When I came back out, everyone was seated comfortably, waiting, saying nothing. I sat in a rocking chair and waited also.

A few minutes later the same maid came in with a tea tray that included a tin of assorted cookies—she knew Carlo Baron well enough to bring him an insulated thermos of coffee and a cup. She poured the coffee for him and he nodded absently, then returned to staring at the wall. Angie poured three cups of tea and offered a plate of cookies. I was surprised to find I wanted one. They were very good cookies. Jerry sat stiffly and refused all nourishment.

I had finished my cookie and taken a few sips of tea when Arthur Terhune arrived.

A rthur nodded to the Barons and Jerry. He didn't bother to nod at me. His expression indicated that he had suspected to see me along with trouble. "Sorry about this," he indicated his khaki work pants, shirt, and boots crusted with dirt. "You said come over. I didn't stop to change."

"Sit down." Baron gestured to a straight wooden chair. I noticed that he had directed Arthur to the one chair in the room that couldn't be easily soiled. "Jerry, go ahead."

Jerry sat up even straighter and began to talk hesitantly. "I been following Steve—for Angie's sake. You know what he was like." He appealed to Arthur, who said nothing, and did not even indicate he had heard.

"As long as he was treating her okay, I left them alone. But when I found out he was cheating, I kept an eye on him when he went out at night. Angie loved him. I didn't want him to hurt her, but I couldn't think of any way to stop him. So I watched him. It was late, but I saw you, Mr. Terhune arguing with Steve. You killed him up on that hill there, took him down and put him in the wine barrel."

Terhune shook his head. "That makes no sense. I didn't kill Steve, but even if I had, why would I incriminate Wolf? He's been good to us."

A Ton of Trouble

"I did find some of Wolf's private papers up there," I couldn't help but say it.

"It's his own property." Terhune stood up and took a step toward Jerry. "Wolf's papers could have come from trash or anywhere. But he never went near that hill except when there were events there. He hadn't been up there in months."

Jerry faced Terhune as if he half expected to be hit. "I didn't see Wolf there, I saw you, Mr. Terhune."

"But you never told anyone?" Carlo Baron asked.

Jerry looked at his shoes. "I wasn't supposed to be there. I didn't want to get in trouble." He slowly looked up and met Carlo Baron's eyes. "I don't care about me, but if I got in trouble who would watch out for Angela?"

"You're not going to take Jerry's word for this, are you?" Terhune sat down, shaking his head. "I admit, I argued with the little bastard. I caught Steve trying to talk to my daughter. She met him at that gazebo up there. She was a damn fool to even talk to him. He fed her some lies about getting back together again and got her to steal some papers from Wolf's office, ungrateful girl. But the stuff she brought him was just gibberish and he told her as much."

Terhune shrugged. "Steve wasn't impressed. He was trying to get Sylvia to steal more pertinent papers. I followed her up there and told him to leave her alone. I had told him before never to talk to her. I hated him for what he did to Sylvia. But I never laid a hand on him. He was alive when he left. If you were following him, you'd know that."

"Give it up, Arthur," Carlo Baron said softly. "We know Steve was involved with some drug cartel."

"What?" If Terhune was faking his shock, he deserved an award for best actor.

Carlo shook his head sadly. "I'm not even going to ask

whether he might have got your daughter involved in that. You're the best wine master I could ever hope to have. If there was any way to save your skin, I would, for your family's sake. Hell, I'd do it just to keep you out of prison and making wine— even if you weren't working for me. I respect your artistry. But I can't let you get away with killing my son-in-law. I run a legitimate operation here. Any of the old connections I have are informal and mostly social these days. But I can't let people disrespect my immediate family. The easiest thing is to just turn you in to the cops. I know he was a blackmailing, cheating son-of-a-bitch, and I owe you one for getting him permanently out of my daughter's life before he knocked her up and complicated everything." He leaned toward Terhune and placed a hand on his arm, "You didn't hear this, understand me? But I'll pay for your lawyers and whatever Sylvia needs—treatment, medicine, whatever. I'll make sure she has it."

Terhune stared at him.

Baron nodded as if they had all struck an agreement, "Whatever she wants. I'll take care of her."

"The way you took care of your daughter—by throwing money at her?" Arthur said in a tone halfway between a growl and a whisper. "I'm not for sale and I won't go to jail to protect your family."

"Come on, Arthur, we know you did it. Jerry said so."

"Two problems here," I said.

"What?" Carlo Baron turned to me with the attitude of a man who is about to swat an annoying insect.

"First there's the cocaine in the Port-a-Pottie on the hill-top."

"So what? Steve could have hid it there," Carlo said, looking at Jerry uncertainly.

"Yeah, he did, I saw him," Jerry said quickly.

"Well, the police might believe that," I said. "But what about Elmira Jones, the neighbor who saw a very large woman and a tall man near those barrels that night?"

"A ninety-year-old broad with glaucoma." Carlo dismissed her.

"She may have glaucoma, but her vision is still twenty-twenty. Her eye doctor told that to Thelma's lawyer. She didn't pick Thelma out of a lineup, but it would be interesting to see if she might be able to identify your wife, Mr. Baron. You didn't mention Angela being there in your story, Jerry, why not?"

Jerry blinked and examined the carpet. Baron moved back into the room, "What is it, Jerry?" He turned to his wife, his voice sank to a whisper. "Angela? You were at that man's house?"

"It's not what you think, Carlo. Jerry and I just put Steve's body in the barrel."

"Then who killed him and where?"

"I killed him." The elder Mrs. Baron walked in through the patio door, wearing a sweater this time and carrying her gardening coverall and gloves.

"It was late afternoon and I was done gardening when I came into that patio there. I come in from time to time to see what my daughter-in-law is up to. She's usually fooling around on that computer. You know how when you stand on the patio you can hear what happens inside? Angela had called Steve in and she asked him to treat little Angie better. He said he didn't have to and he threatened to tell Carlo about Angela's flirtation with that Lambert fool." She snorted. "Then Steve said he was divorcing my granddaughter to marry his little office bimbo. He got in bad with some gangsters. No one we know, drug people. Mexicans." She sniffed.

"He was letting them store drugs in different rental units—

keeping those properties off the market and saying they were being renovated. Stealing from his family and he was stealing from the gangsters, too. So he was going to take his little receptionist and run away. The son-in-law business was too tough for him, I guess."

She took off her bifocals and examined the silver beads that held them round her neck. "We have never had a divorce in this family. And we never will. I came in here to tell him that, but before I could say one word, Angela explained it to him. He just laughed and said no one could stop him from divorcing little Angie. He said he'd hidden drugs in Angie's belongings and he could get her arrested with one phone call."

She shook her head. "I was standing in the garden, so I put my gloves back on and picked up a rock and marched in there. He was sitting in the chair you're sitting in, Miss Fuller. He had his legs crossed, and he was telling my daughter-in-law he was going to ruin my granddaughter's life. Humiliate our whole family. I hit him on the back of the head with the rock. He never even heard me walk up behind him. Knocked him out."

"Mother—"

"Shut up, Angie."

Angela Baron flinched, and I could see she was shocked at what her mother-in-law had said, but it was the shock of hearing someone tell the truth when it is least expected.

"I told Angie to go get Jerry because she's a weak one. I didn't want her to see what I was going to do." The old lady took a coil of twine out of her pocket. "I had garden twine and plant stakes in my coverall, like I usually do. So I threw a length of garden twine around the little coward's neck and pulled him back in the rocking chair off his feet. Like this!"

Before anyone could move, she had walked up behind me and looped the twine around my neck.

A Ton of Trouble

"Hey!" I reached back, but she rocked the chair so that I couldn't move. Out of the corner of my eye I could see the Barons, Jerry, and Arthur standing there frozen, staring.

Mrs. Baron's voice continued from behind me. "He was out cold. Didn't even struggle. I twisted the twine around the plant stake and kept on twisting. Like this, see?" The stake scratched against the canvas pocket as she pulled it out of her apron. The noose around my neck tightened and the rocking chair was rocked back.

I felt my feet leave the floor. She had rocked the chair so that she was holding me against the back of the chair. I could smell her clove gum. Her arms trembled a little.

"I just held it twisted up tight," she said next to my ear. "I held him against the chair."

I grabbed at the cord, but she had twisted it tight. No one was coming to my rescue. They all seemed to be in shock. The room grew dim.

"Harder to kill than a chicken but not as hard as a calf," Mrs. Baron said in my ear.

I lowered my arms onto the chair arms and desperately tried to rock forward, but the chair was too far back on its rocker, and my weight combined with her wiry hundred pounds was holding it back. I threw my legs up and leaned farther back, rocking the chair over backward. The chair, Mrs. Baron, and I all went over.

"Mama!" Carlo Baron rushed to help his mother.

Mrs. Baron dropped the twine as she fell and I dug it out of my throat, taking big gasps of air and choking. I crawled over the side of the chair and wound up on my hands and knees breathing heavily and watching Carlo and Jerry help her up.

"Are you all right, Mama?"

"Thank you son, I'm a little bruised, is all." Her hard brown eyes rested on me. "If I'd had that rock you'd have been dead, missy. Angela took it when she got rid of the body. She came back with Jerry and just stood there staring at Steve's body. Big cow. I told her he'd had a heart attack and she'd better make herself useful. Get Jerry and take the body over to Lambert's overnight. Put it somewhere easy to find. Steve had been over there so often, let them get the blame. It might even make him sell his land if he got in enough trouble." She winked genially and I realized she was quite mad.

"I told her she had to go through all of little Angie's things, find the drugs and get rid of them. That's when Jerry told me he had found some drugs. Isn't that right, Jerry?"

"Jerry?" Carlo looked up at the huge man, who was twisting his hands as if in physical pain.

"What do you want me to say? I'll say whatever you want."

"Of course you will," Mrs. Baron said, patting Jerry's arm. "You're a loyal friend."

"I told the two of them to wait till it got fully dark to take the body away. Then I went back to gardening."

"Angela, is this true?" Carlo turned to his wife.

We all looked at Angela. She nodded.

Carlo Baron collapsed into a chair, staring at his mother. "You asked Angie to do that? Why didn't you come to me?"

"You, Carlo? Your hands have always been clean. Angela—she understands how important it is to protect little Angie. Thank God, little Angie was staying with her cousin in San Francisco. Jerry, he's not smart. But he'd already found the cocaine, hadn't you, child?"

Jerry nodded reluctantly. "When I changed a flat tire on Angie's car—the SL, I tried to bounce the spare and it was too heavy. I found the drugs hidden there—must have been thirty pounds. I took the tire over to the trunk of the car I was driving—the big Mercedes. I hid it there until I could hide it somewhere off the property."

"You didn't tell me?" Carlo appeared in shock.

"I didn't have time. But Mrs. Baron called me to get rid of the body, I told her and she suggested we put it in the Port-a-Pottie up on the hill at Mr. Lambert's."

The senior Mrs. Baron nodded approvingly. "I knew you would want to protect little Angie, dear."

Jerry nodded.

"That didn't solve your problem, though did it? And now we know," I said to Mrs. Baron, rubbing my injured throat.

"You won't live to tell anyone else," she said, taking out a small, pearl-handled revolver.

"You're going to kill someone with that?" Arthur Terhune said, staring.

"I've got six bullets. You first." She fired and Arthur staggered backward.

"Put down the gun, Mama, you don't know what you're doing." Carlo advanced toward his mother, but Mrs. Baron pulled back the hammer again and turned toward me.

There was a rush of heavy footsteps in the hall, and when she hesitated I scrambled to my feet and shoved the fallen rocking chair out of the way. A moment later the door was smashed in and I saw armed gunmen coming through the fence, onto the patio, and through the patio door. "Police. Everybody down on the floor."

Carlo Baron wrestled his mother to the floor, just as her revolver fired again.

I was close to the floor already, so I rolled onto my stomach and hugged the carpet. Glancing up, I saw the "FBI" stenciled on the back of the jackets as the officers went from person to person checking for injuries. One man stayed crouching by Arthur and thumbed a two-way radio. "One injury, we need a medical unit."

Out of my line of vision, I heard a woman's voice say, "This old lady's bleeding out."

I was relieved to notice that none of the men here were the men who had taken me out of the condo in San Francisco. One man helped me to my feet and escorted me out of the house, through a crowd of police officers in body armor, bristling with communication gear. Another man in a suit rather than a uniform, a two-way radio crackling in his hand, appeared to be at the center of the whirlwind. Standing next to him and looking as disreputable as ever were Harvey Dowd and Wally Ramos.

Harvey gestured me over. "Would you like to sit in my car for a minute and have some coffee and donuts? I'll fill you in."

"Don't go away, we'll need to talk to you," the man with the two-way radio said.

A Ton of Trouble

"Wouldn't dream of it. But I'm sure the lady needs to sit down." Harvey guided me through a forest of official police vehicles, over to a battered old Ford. I sat in the passenger side while Harry leaned on the door and Wally leaned against the side of the car.

"It was our turn for doughnuts." Wally offered me the box and I took one, feeling suddenly ravenous as the adrenaline began to wear off.

"We were following that strange woman with the rifle and damned if she didn't start shooting up that building on Pine when you came out." Wally put the box on top of the car, produced a plastic foam cup and a thermos of coffee from the backseat. He poured me a cup.

"Took us a while to get the police to understand that they were dealing with a sniper and a bunch of drug dealers, because the security guard in San Francisco kept saying they were with the FBI." Wally helped himself to a doughnut and handed the box to Harvey.

"But we told them who the lady was and what we found out about the guys who went into your condo." Harvey took a doughnut also and put the box back on the roof of the car.

"What did you find out?"

"They were some pretty highly connected drug dealers who were doing business with Steve Farquar." Wally had finished his doughnut and was now pouring himself some coffee. "He started as a juvenile delinquent and chemist, making his own crystal meth, and he got some connections with cocaine importers."

"It turned out Steve was renting the Baron Realty properties out at a high rate to dealers for very short-term safe houses," Harvey said.

"They would bring the drug shipments in by disguising

themselves as workmen doing repairs on the houses and apartment buildings. Then they'd move on to the next place. That was working fine until Steve got greedy—he wanted to advance in their organization, but the only thing he had to offer was his father-in-law's property. He told them he wanted to make more money so he could run off with his little girlfriend. He was on his way out and he knew it, so he stole one of their shipments. But someone else killed him before the dealers could track him down to ask him where their shipment was hidden."

"That must have been why they killed Monty down in Southern California," I mused.

"It must be quite a lot of dope. They probably would have killed that Steve guy if someone else hadn't got to him first."

"His wife's grandmother killed him." I realized my coffee had gone cold in my hands, but I took a drink, anyway.

Harvey took a drink of his own coffee. "Got to watch those old ladies."

Wally nodded sagely. "Anyway, we had a pretty good idea that the guy driving the Mercedes was connected to the Baron family. So we told the police and headed on up here ourselves. They were watching the place already. When we told them what happened they were going to move in to look for you. But they heard gunfire, so they went inside a lot quicker." He held out his hands, slopping a little coffee from the cup in his hand onto the gravel.

"Thank you," I said fervently.

41

It was two days later when Mrs. Madrone called me into her office. She had my report on her desk. As well as the *San Francisco Chronicle*. She tapped a front-page article. The headline read, SNIPER TIED TO ANTI-ABORTION BABY MILL—RACISM CHARGED.

"Did you alert the newspapers to this?"

"No, ma'am." I had been too busy talking to the police to talk to any reporters, although I had taken a few minutes to read the article.

"I do apologize about any damage done to the Pine Street building."

"That's hardly your fault." Mrs. Madrone smiled faintly. "I think I may advise Nanette Archambault that the repair of the Pine Street property her associate damaged has absorbed any money we might have considered donating to her clinics. Of course, we are insured—and fortunately no people were injured—there. I understand the Baron family in Sonoma County was not so fortunate."

"Yes. The elder Mrs. Baron died by her own gun. It was an accident, in that she was trying to shoot me at the time."

Mrs. Madrone shook her head. "I understand they found large quantities of drugs on their property?"

"Steve Farquar, the man stuffed in the wine barrel, had stashed several million dollars worth of cocaine on his father-in-law's property and also in his wife's Mercedes sports car. I think he meant to send the dealers after her as a diversion."

"Josephine, you lead much too stimulating a life. I encourage you to take some time off for the holidays."

"Yes, ma'am. I'm going back to Seattle, if you can spare me for a few weeks."

"Yes. Go ahead and go. I'll be visiting friends in Tuscany over the holidays."

Mulligan was glad to see me, although perhaps a little daunted when he saw that I had not only brought a case of Lambert's Lair wines, but a stack of Wolf Lambert's videos.

"What happened to your friend Thelma?"

"Mrs. Baron admitted she killed Steve Farquar rather than let him divorce her granddaughter. I don't know if they're going to charge Angela Baron and Jerry Park for moving the body. Thelma was cleared of all suspicion in the murder. She's moving back in with Wolf. I think he's going to help her with her web site."

"Are you going to watch all those videos?" he asked.

"These are supposed to be very good."

He looked at the covers, which were more tasteful than the *Big, Bad Biker Babes* cover. When he had finished looking at them, he handed them back to me and I put them in the box and put the box next to the VCR.

"You don't want to watch them right now?" he asked.

I smiled at him. "Curious?"

"I might be."

"Well, I'm taking a couple of weeks off. I was thinking of

saving them for a rainy day—or maybe a rainy night if I can arrange for suitable companionship."

"This is Seattle. It rains all the time."

I couldn't argue with that.